Sahara Blue

Jan Irving

Dreamspinner Press

Published by
Dreamspinner Press
4760 Preston Road
Suite 244-149
Frisco, TX 75034
http://www.dreamspinnerpress.com/

Sahara Blue

Cover Art by Paul Richmond   http://www.paulrichmondstudio.com

ISBN: 978-1-61581-654-5

Printed in the United States of America
First Edition
November, 2010

eBook edition available
eBook ISBN: 978-1-61581-655-2

I wrote the first half of this story in a rush of excitement but then suffered a blood clot that made me leave it for more than half a year. By the time I got back to it, fortunately after embarking on some wonderful changes such as working with yoga, I didn't know what to do with it. But then I showed it to Jambrea Jo Jones, who told me she'd love to see more. With her help and that of my first readers, I completed this story, for me and for them and for any readers who wanted to know more about Sahara Blue and his Seth.

When I let go of what I am, I become what I might be.

— Lao-Tzu

Prologue

BEYOND the light from the streetlamp, the tall, muscular man ran a hand over the black mask concealing his face. He looked at the watch that had survived jungle duty, a Luminox 3001.

Right on time, shopkeeper Seth Hollis turned out the lights downstairs in his fabric and dye store. Seeing him, the man's heart rate picked up, and when no traffic appeared, he crossed the street, heading for the fire escape he'd reconnoitered previously. He pulled himself up easily and climbed to the second floor. There was a window surrounded by a traditional Victorian brick frame which looked into Seth Hollis's hallway.

Patient, the man crouched.

Finally, his vigil was rewarded: Hollis walked by, barefoot and wearing only a sarong and a pair of glasses, his brown curly hair smoothed from a fresh shower.

"Gotcha, Lotus," the man whispered.

Chapter One

NUDE except for the dangling silver chain holding woven, vivid blue beads that fell between his nipples, Sahara Blue Drummond leaned in front of his floor-to-ceiling windows, looking out at sea.

He'd opened one of them so the salt air breeze, so familiar to him, could soothe his senses, but it had so far failed, leaving him to prowl his living room... restless.

Hard.

His body was aching for the teasing body of one man—Lotus, the enigmatic blogger who put up alluring stories online that stirred Sahara.

"He's just a fantasy," Sahara muttered to himself. But he smiled as he remembered a recent exchange they'd shared on the blog when Lotus had teased him about his name—Sahara Blue. It did sound made-up, but it was what his hippie late-seventies mom had come up with.

He sighed. There were moments when he felt close to Lotus, as if they had a real connection, but then there were times like this when Sahara was confronted with how alone he was. He needed more. He needed a man in the flesh, not an online crush.

Sahara touched a palm to cool glass, his gaze unfocused but his body ready, always ready for the unexpected. He whirled around suddenly, left leg going up with enough force to break someone's neck. With perfect control, he lowered it, hands fisted at his sides.

He was keyed up tonight, riding adrenaline the way he had when he'd been an active SEAL. For some reason, the past few days, he'd felt as if someone was watching him. It was giving him an itch between the shoulders and making him want to go out hunting for the reason his nerves were buzzing; it better not be someone planning on hurting Toby and Jared again, friends who lived in a floating home nearby, because he was a man of his word and he'd warned Toby's ex to leave them both alone.

But his restlessness was more than his tingling spider senses. After reading another of Lotus's scorching stories, all Sahara had was his right hand for relief, something all too common. When was the last time he'd thrust into a tight ass, fucking a trick in an alley somewhere? And even that wasn't satisfying because as much as he yearned to bury his face against someone's neck, to talk to him, he was always silent, unable to say the right thing.

His body burned for relief, yet he didn't want only that. Being around Toby and Jared lately was turning him into a grump. He could see the love flowing free between them, could practically feel the heat wave when they looked at each other. Sometimes he was allowed a little taste of play with them, but lately it had only made it harder for him, making him ache for familiar arms around him. He wanted someone in his bed, not just to take his cock, but to be there so he could nestle his head into a warm neck and listen to the throb of a beating heart.

On nights like tonight, when he had the shakes, it was worse. He felt hollowed out, unable to sleep. But he never wanted anyone to see him, to touch him, when he was this wired. Maybe that was part of why Lotus had become his obsession; he was safe.

Sahara returned to his study to open a file a computer-savvy friend of his had made of specially enhanced photographs taken from Lotus's blog. He'd become convinced some time ago that Lotus actually put up pictures of himself on his blog. It seemed that of all Lotus's myriad admirers, only Sahara had sensed this. Sometimes, late at night, it seemed as if it were some kind of message meant for him alone, as if Lotus's true reason for writing in his online diary was to attract *Sahara's* attention.

"Yeah, right." Sahara shook his head now, dismissing the idea. That had to be nuts, as well as somewhat arrogant on his part. But his bones, his body, felt some kind of primal tie to Lotus, as if the man were meant to be his. Even knowing how crazy it was, he couldn't seem to shake the feeling.

He looked at a picture, creased from his touch, of a young man with a thick, beautiful cock, partially erect, tied with rough hemp rope to a tree. His soft, brown, curly hair obscured his face, tilted away from the camera, but his sad, bowed lips were visible.

How often had Sahara stared at those lips, imagining them on his nipples while he cried out and clenched his hands in that tumbled hair? Lotus wouldn't be sad if he were in Sahara's bed. He'd be hot, sweaty, satisfied... smiling.

Sahara remembered a few months ago when he'd first gotten the guts to finally comment on Lotus's blog, typing, *Are you as lonely as I am?*

And Lotus had replied, *I am very lonely.*

"Huh," Sahara grunted now. "Aren't we a pair?" Abandoning the photos, Sahara returned to his living room. If he had been the one to take that picture of Lotus tied to a tree, he would have kissed him while he was trussed up, taking his time to lick and savor. He couldn't remember the last time he'd actually kissed anyone! And his hand would be wrapped around Lotus's trapped cock, playing with it until Lotus begged Sahara to let him come.

Shit, they'd both enjoy it, and he'd know Lotus was his when his come spattered against Sahara's legs.

He wanted Lotus. He wanted him under him, in his bed, looking into Sahara's eyes as Sahara kissed him, mounted him.

WEARING an *Ikat*-patterned sarong and nothing else, Seth Hollis rolled his shoulders to release the day's tension as he walked around his darkened shop. It was late, but he was restless, his body aching for touch.

He sighed. What else was new?

As he puttered, morose, he retouched the display of natural dyes his shop specialized in, madder, logwood, cutch, cochineal.... The custom tins he had made up for his supply store sounded like exotic spices in a marketplace, and that always brought on daydreams of living in another time and being owned by some kind of pasha, of being summoned at night to please him. Of course, Seth would be his favorite, would love lying under him night after night....

Shaking his head at his vivid daydream, he turned each mustard tag-covered product so it was best displayed and then stepped back, pushing his longish brown hair out of his eyes. As he did so, he was caught for a moment by his own very ordinary reflection in a hand-hammered, Mexican, tin-framed mirror. He met his somber brown eyes, only remarkable to some because they hinted at his Japanese grandmother, but the rest of him was merely pale, brown and brown, nondescript like a plain sparrow.

He glanced away, thinking that Sahara Blue, the man who prodded him on his blog, would never go for such a mousy boy-next-door type. He probably expected someone really cut, with blond good looks—someone teasing and confident and sexy... like Lotus.

Seth burned in the sun, so he enjoyed it safely under an awning or a hat. And he was far from sexually experienced. All his adventures were in his head; at twenty-five, the embarrassing truth was that he was a virgin.

In fact, other than his passion for collecting things from around the world to bring to his shop and selling dyes and various supplies for textile artists, the only interesting thing about him was his alter ego, Lotus.

He looked over at his laptop, sitting on a battered table made of a door from India, one of the furniture products of fair trade he offered in his shop, and wished, not for the first time, that he could somehow make some real contact. At times, he felt like he might have it with

Sahara Blue, but he knew he was kidding himself; it was only the illusion of intimacy that came from sharing things he'd never have the courage to share in real life.

And in real life, a blond, untamed cougar of a man would not take one look at him.

Seth knew this for certain, since he'd sought out his mystery man. There weren't any other men with that strange name in the San Diego area, which Sahara Blue had assured him was real, so it hadn't been hard to find him. In fact, Seth had wondered if Sahara had somehow been daring Lotus to come get him. It would be like the man, who often wrote about how he wanted Lotus.

Sahara Blue Drummond had a floating home a mile from where Seth had his small shop. Seth had waited once by the local wharf market, which sold wraps and other fast foods, and spotted him, vivid blue eyes, tall, muscled, with some kind of azure bead thing hanging around his neck.

He was hot as fuck, stirring Seth's fantasies into high gear. God, what would it be like to belong to such a man?

But no way he'd be interested in a pale, brown sparrow. Seth's stupid ideas about somehow finding a way to approach him evaporated. He was stuck in the persona of Lotus, the only way he'd ever appeal to a man like Sahara.

Seth caught a pathetic *mew* sound from the back door and roused from his apathy. He emptied some of the cream he'd brought in for his coffee that morning into a Japanese bowl and opened the door out back, facing the Dumpster. The kitten's green eyes blinked at him from across the width of the narrow alley. Seth put down the bowl and wished the little creature would trust him enough to come inside. "Well, at least someone needs me," he whispered.

Suddenly a dark man-shape loomed. The kitten fled—

"*Oh!*" Seth relaxed. "Rudy, you scared me!"

Rudy looked around. "The k-kitten gone, Seth?" He was a tall man with a dark mustache and goatee who worked a few shops down in the grocery where Seth got his fresh fruits and vegetables. According to local shopkeepers' gossip, Rudy had spent some time in South America, and when he'd come back, he hadn't been the same person. He worked hard but was shy around people. Seth had always felt a kinship with him.

His friend Karen referred to him as another of Seth's strays, as much as the kitten.

"No, I'm afraid he's gone, but I'll leave the milk, Rudy," Seth reassured. "He'll come back."

Rudy's pale eyes fell from Seth's. He nodded before continuing down the alley, hands dug deep in his pockets.

Seth waited a few more minutes for the kitten to possibly make another appearance but when it didn't return he returned to his shop, closing and locking the back door behind him.

GIVING up on sleep, Sahara decided to go for a run. He did it often, uphill on beach dunes being one of his favorite ways to keep in shape. He could still run like the wind, though with his head injuries, he'd never be what he had been again.

In fact, his head was pounding now from one of his damned headaches. He paused, wearing a T-shirt and shorts in preparation for his workout, and debated taking something for it. But he hated to admit any weakness. He could live with pain. How else could he have become a SEAL in the first place?

He headed out, deciding to run past some of the shops in the streets above where he lived. Maybe he'd find something for his home so it wouldn't be so barren. Jared and Toby's nest was like a jewel case, and sometimes he found himself wishing he had a few nice things in his own place... but he was fucking useless at that kind of thing, almost as bad as when he tried to open up and say something to pick up some cute guy. Instead, he found himself treating his dates like prey, pulling them into the shadows behind a club when his body was screaming for release and burning out his passion inside them.

Now, lacking the sex his body ached for, lacking any kind of partner, he ran down the pier, seeing that Toby and Jared's bedroom light was on. His throat tightened. He wondered what they were doing together. Was Jared teaching Toby more about meditation? Or were they making slow love with the sea air touching their sweating bodies as they kissed and moved together? Shit. It was tough being the single dude around that pair.

FINALLY, Seth decided he needed to head upstairs to bed. Tomorrow was Saturday, and it could be busy, so he'd have to be alert for his customers, both on the website he maintained and in his shop. Plus, now that Thanksgiving was over, the holiday shoppers would begin to show up. He'd have to give some thought to displays to showcase gift-giving.

Yet he knew he probably wouldn't sleep right away. Instead, he'd lie awake and imagine yet another scenario where he met his dream man, Sahara Blue, and somehow Sahara wanted him, despite Seth's mundane looks and shy personality.

Feeling rather wistful, he imagined a storyline in which he was a slave in a pirate's space ship and Sahara Blue was an intergalactic cop who intercepted illegal cargo. When he came across the ship where slave-Seth was a prisoner, he freed everyone, of course, since he was a hero, but Seth would be too traumatized after his experiences to be left on his own, so Sahara kept him on his ship, and of course Seth would have trouble sleeping through the night so the hot futuristic cop let him into his bed, holding him close to his hard body, keeping him safe.

Mmmmm.

Seth took a deep breath, since it didn't take much to arouse him, thinking of Sahara. He really had to get over his crush on the other man. It wasn't real. It could never be real.

Shattering glass—

Heart pounding, Seth whirled around, seeing in the light from the street a spiderweb of splintered shards glinting in the center of his shop window.

Someone had broken it!

He hesitated, wanting to investigate but suddenly afraid. Should he go upstairs and call someone? His hand clenched on the stair rail. Sometimes at night, tough characters roamed this part of town, which was partly why the rent was so reasonable, allowing Seth to live above his shop.

As he watched, a tall figure moved in front of his window.

SAHARA BLUE had reached a good pace, body on autopilot as his mind roamed free. His muscles had a burn going, and he liked the feel of the air pumping through his lungs, of how strong his arms and legs felt. He knew he could keep this pace up for another half-hour before his body would start to shake and he'd have to ease down.

His face blurred past him in shop windows. Lingerie, leather belts and jackets, some strangely shaped lamps in a lighting store that reminded him of one of the futuristic worlds imaginative Lotus sometimes wrote about.

Lotus…. The thought of the man haunting him made Sahara's pace slow, so he was walking, hands on his hips, his shirt and shorts sticking to his hot, damp body despite the cooler, early December night air.

Something ahead caught his eye. A dark figure ran past a shop window ahead, and glass shattered.

Sniper. Gunshot.

Heart pounding, Sahara dropped, checking out the gray outlines of buildings until this reality slowly righted itself over his instinctive one.

No. No, this wasn't his past, which he couldn't remember except in sunshine and shadow patchwork. This was just some punk who broke a window.

Shaking, Sahara regained his feet, seeing that in the time it had taken him to fight off the flashback, the figure had disappeared.

He had to make sure no one was hurt by the glass, call it in to the cops…. He fished out his BlackBerry and headed for the vandalized shop.

SETH was frozen by the stairs when a soft voice called out, "Are you all right in there?"

Shit! Whoever it was had to have eyes like a cat, to make him out. He took a deep breath, still hesitant to move forward into the light from the street.

"Look, I can see you back there. I just called the cops." The figure raised a BlackBerry. "I'll stay out here until they get here."

The voice was strong, male, concerned. Seth was lured a little closer, so he eased to the front of his shop.

The man had his back turned now, his head down. He was wearing shorts and a T-shirt that clung to lean muscle and a high, perfect ass. His legs had sandy hairs, and his running shoes were black pull-ons.

As if feeling Seth's gaze, the stranger looked up, and familiar, killer blue eyes stabbed into the shadows, looking into Seth.

It was Sahara Blue.

Chapter Two

"IT'S you," Seth whispered.

Sahara immediately frowned at him. "Are you all right? Did some of the glass hit you? I have experience with first aid…." He shoved back some sandy blond hair off his forehead, looking impatient, as if it was hard for him not to demand Seth let him in his shop so he could take care of him.

Seth blinked, feeling spacey. He'd just been thinking of this man, his fantasy man, and suddenly he was right there, while glass glittered between them. The moment felt oddly significant.

"You sound like you want to take care of me," Seth noted wryly, covering for the way his throat tightened. He ducked his head. God, he was acting like a total dweeb, but he'd lived fantasies of Sahara Blue so much in his head that he felt exposed.

Sahara growled, "Dude, you're not making a lot of sense."

"I know that!" Seth snapped back, color flushing his cheeks. "Hello, not every night my shop window gets smashed."

"Huh, well, now you seem a little better." Sahara raised his brows.

"Thank you." Seth knew defiance was written on his face, but suddenly he was pissed. Glass breaking, and then here was Sahara, and Seth didn't want to meet him.

Sahara put his hands on his hips. "Are you going to let me in or not?"

Seth hesitated for a moment and then drifted numbly to his door, switching off the alarm and then unlatching the locks. Sahara pushed inside, sneakers crunching over glass as he headed to investigate.

"You're not a cop."

Ignoring Seth's censure, Sahara knelt beside a large rock, something that Seth had entirely missed.

"Oh, God," he repeated, realizing that must be what had been tossed through the glass.

"There's a piece of paper tied to it, but I better leave it for the cops to take a look," Sahara noted absently before looking up at Seth. "Hey." His voice softened, and he climbed smoothly to his feet, moving toward Seth with easy grace. His hair was dripping from his exercise, shoved back in sweaty peaks around his face. His clothes were still damp from his run, gloving hard muscle like a loving hand.

"I'm Sahara Blue," Sahara introduced himself, unaware that Seth was fully aware of who he was.

"Seth Hollis," Seth muttered. He stuck out his hand, and Sahara took it, squeezing it gently for a moment and making Seth's pulse race.

Seth's gaze dropped to Sahara's crotch. He blushed at how obvious a tell that was and looked away. He was practically licking the man! But he wanted to do just that.

"It's all right," Sahara reassured. "I'll stay until the cops get here."

Seth swallowed dryly, struck by Sahara's protectiveness. He sensed that if the other man knew him better, he might give him a reassuring hug. Shit! "I… was pretty shaken up," he admitted. "I've been at this location for three years and nothing like this has ever happened."

"Mmmm, something sudden like this can really be scary. Listen… maybe you should put on some clothes?" Sahara raised a sandy brow, and Seth felt immediately self-conscious. He was wearing nothing but a sarong around his slight waist, exposing his slender chest and pale skin, his bare feet.

"Fuck, you cut yourself!" Before Seth could blink, Sahara charged closer and swung Seth into his arms. Blood dripped from Seth's left foot, where he must have stepped on the slender shards. He'd been so focused on Sahara, he hadn't noticed.

He clutched Sahara's arms, staring into eyes that were even more vivid close up, the same color as the azure-beaded pendant that Sahara wore around his neck. Seth had been intrigued by the distinctive necklace since he'd first glimpsed it. "You should put me down!" he reproved. "I'm not helpless, Sahara."

Sahara ignored him. "Got a sink close by where I can clean you up with a first-aid kit?"

"And I repeat, I'm perfectly capable of taking care of myself!" Seth gritted.

"Yeah, perfectly capable of hurting yourself. I can see that for myself," Sahara noted.

He tried to glare Seth into submission, but Seth only glared back. Sahara's face softened, and one callused thumb stroked Seth's arm, which wasn't muscled like the ones on the man holding him, but just… arm. Seth had tried working out, but it never seemed to take. No more than eating a lot of food to try to bulk up. He'd been a skinny mouse all his life.

"Let me take care of you," Sahara whispered, his eyes suddenly intense on Seth's. "It's kind of who I am."

Seth dropped his gaze, shrugging. Fine. But his heart was pounding in his ears. He was enveloped by Sahara, pressed close to the hard planes of his chest, close enough to smell the musk of his workout. He had a vision of himself burying his face between Sahara's legs and rubbing gently against his pubic hair.

Crap! He'd better not let his thoughts get out of control. He was stiffening, and the silky fabric of the sarong was hardly going to conceal that. He directed in a gruff voice, "Bathroom's up those stairs. Just put me on the riser and I'll head up if you wait for the cops."

"I'll hear them when they get here," Sahara contradicted. Instead of obeying Seth's edict, he carried him, taking the stairs two at a time, easy, not even breathing hard.

Unlike Seth, who thought he'd pass out. "You're jolting me around like a sack of flour!" he growled.

Sahara's eyes widened, and for the very first time, Seth saw uncertainty there. It surprised him, since he hadn't expected that. Why would such a hot guy feel it? Then Sahara scowled. "Just do what you're told."

Seth gaped. Then he said crossly, "I'd never hire *you* to work in my shop. You don't know how to treat people."

Sahara only muttered something under his breath, carrying Seth gently into the first room at the top of the stairs, which was Seth's small bathroom. He lowered him gently onto the john. "Do you have supplies to clean up something like this?" Sahara asked, lifting Seth's slender foot into the cup of his warm, callused hands. One finger ran over Seth's heel, making him shiver.

In the bathroom mirror, Seth caught a glimpse of himself: high color in his cheeks, wide, outraged brown eyes and hard nipples, beading at Sahara's touch. He hoped the other man didn't notice. "In the cabinet under the sink," he said.

Sahara had to bend down to reach the supplies, giving Seth a look at the tangled sandy hair falling away from the skin at the nape of his neck, a slightly paler color than the rest of his tanned body, reminding Seth for some reason of the inside of an oyster shell.

He wanted to press his lips against that skin.

Instead, he chewed on them, wrestling with his feelings. He couldn't bear to be rejected by this man in real life. He had to hide what he was feeling, crawl safely into his shell. Already he was trembling from being so close to him. It sucked, being inexperienced.

"You're cold," Sahara said, noticing immediately that Seth had the shakes. He took Seth's hands in his and then lifted his wet T-shirt, placing Seth's cold palms flat against his skin. Sahara's body was hot from his run, like touching a stallion after a race.

"Uh...." Seth couldn't resist flexing his fingers a little in an almost-caress. This was as close as he'd ever come to another man!

Sahara's sharp blue eyes zeroed in on his face, studying him. He whispered, "You want me."

Seth jerked his hands away.

There was a pause, and he had the strange impression that Sahara was frustrated, as if seeking something to say. But what could he say after exposing Seth's pathetic want so baldly?

"Sit still, little one," Sahara finally ordered, lifting Seth's foot so he could take a closer look. "Um, there's a sliver there. Do you want to go see a doc, or do you trust me to remove it?"

Seth's gaze flew to Sahara's impassive face. He was waiting patiently, as if he hadn't said those embarrassing words. Seth swallowed thickly. "I'd rather you take it out."

Sahara caressed Seth's foot, as if approving of his choice. Seth's lips parted as he stared into those killer blue eyes. He could see himself reflected in the dark pupils.

"Okay, I'll use the tweezers and then some of the alcohol to clean it up," Sahara offered, his shoulders relaxing as if he was comfortable with Seth allowing him to completely take charge. "Then I can bandage it."

Seth nodded, not knowing what to say. He was giving over control of his body to this man, even if it was just a sliver, but it felt huge to him, so he was hypersensitive to every touch.

Using the tweezers and bending close, Sahara pulled the sliver out in one smooth try. His lips quirked at Seth's wide-eyed look. "I wouldn't hurt you," he said, his words seeming to have some kind of double meaning. "I, uh, was a medic on my team."

"Uh-huh." Seth continued to stare at Sahara, and the other man flushed.

A swab with the alcohol, and then he put a bandage on the puncture. He stood, towering over Seth in the tiny space. "Where are your shoes and clothing?"

Seth blinked. "Um, in my closet. Next room."

Sahara nodded coolly, and then, as if he had every right to do it, he disappeared, leaving a dazed Seth behind. It seemed he truly was in his fantasy man's hands.

Most unsettling of all, Sahara was living up to the fantasy.

SAHARA quickly rooted through Seth's closet, finding a pair of shorts and a pale blue T-shirt with hibiscus flowers on it. There were also some brown leather sandals he didn't think would hurt the sore foot.

As he did, he grumbled to himself about how he'd come out with something so... primal to the other man. Right away, as if catching some kind of scent, he'd known Seth was gay. But to tell Seth that he wanted Sahara... Sahara guessed that wasn't done. Why did he turn into Tarzan when he was around a guy he liked?

Of course, Seth wearing nothing but that sexy little sarong would push a man. All the time Sahara had been taking care of him, he'd been aware how easy it would be to lift up the cloth, spread Seth's legs, and mount him.

He closed his eyes for a moment, holding up Seth's T-shirt to take a whiff of the other man's scent. Behind his sealed lids, he could imagine himself back in the little bathroom, reflected in the bathroom mirror along with Seth. Seth's body braced as he accepted Sahara pounding into him.

Shit, he had no idea why he was reacting like this! It wasn't like Seth was asking for it. He seemed very shy. Sahara liked his brown, tilted eyes, expressive as they'd held his. He liked his pale skin that was translucent so Sahara could make out the pattern of veins, and he even liked the spark of defiance when he got too bossy with Seth.

But what he'd really like was to push Seth against any flat surface and thrust into him.

"YOU'LL need to strip," Sahara announced as soon as he reappeared with Seth's clothing.

Seth's heart jumped. "Uh."

Sahara stared at him for a sustained moment. "I'll turn my back," he offered silkily.

That tone seemed to wrap around Seth's cock, teasing him. He nodded, throat too tight to speak. He wrote all kinds of erotic stories on his blog, even had his friend Karen, an amateur photographer, take pictures of him sometimes in the nude, but he'd never been alone with another man in his bathroom before. He felt awkward, unable to behave like it was no big deal.

As soon as Sahara's lean back was to him, Seth dropped his sarong quickly and tugged on his shorts. He'd be commando, but they would do a better job of containing his embarrassing reaction to Sahara's care. He next pulled on the T-shirt, glad to conceal his unremarkable upper body, which didn't ripple with muscle like Sahara's.

"Okay?" Sahara prodded.

"Yeah, sure," Seth said.

Sahara turned around, sandals still dangling from one hand. He guided Seth back to the john, and while Seth watched, a little shaken by the intimacy of how Sahara had taken over caring for him, he placed them carefully on Seth's feet. "I'll miss that sarong," Sahara said, picking it up off the floor.

"Um." Seth didn't know what he would have said. A firm knock from downstairs interrupted the moment. He jumped, and Sahara squeezed his shoulder. "Easy. That'll be the cops."

"I should get that," Seth said, shoving back his curly hair and trying to put on a businesslike front. This was his shop, and he had to get that mess cleaned up and a new window in there pronto. His busiest day was Saturday, so much so that his friend Karen sometimes came in to spell him for a couple of hours.

Sahara stood aside and let Seth walk past him, but as the bigger man followed on his heels, Seth felt oddly as if he were being pursued. His stomach tightened at the sensation, making him clench his fists. He was conscious again of his own innocence, of his body throbbing, unsatisfied.

He had the feeling that Sahara Blue could satisfy him.

TO SETH'S surprise, Sahara greeted the cop waiting outside the shop door with familiarity. "Officer Martinez," he said, shaking the policeman's hand as the two men exchanged a look that spoke of equality.

Terrific. Watching, Seth wanted to retreat to the shadows, especially when Martinez ran his gaze over Sahara in an inviting fashion. He had dark good looks and warm sherry eyes. He was also someone who was no stranger to a bench press.

Knowing he'd been eclipsed, Seth told himself it was just as well. What could the mouse offer the tiger?

SAHARA knelt next to Officer Martinez as the other man used a pen to gently tease the paper free of a rubber band holding it to the fist-sized rock that had shattered Seth's window. He craned his neck to make out the words spelled out crudely in pasted letters from newspaper.

"*I know... who you are,*" Sahara read aloud. He looked up at Seth, who had his arms wrapped around himself as if chilled, despite the fact that it was warming into morning. It made a protective feeling move through Sahara, so he decided he'd do something about that. Soon. "Any idea what that means?"

Seth shook his head. "None."

Chapter Three

"I CAN'T believe I let you talk me into this!" Seth grumbled to Sahara as he sat down on a wharf bench near Sahara's home. Except he was supposed to pretend he'd never been here, of course. Shit, he hoped he didn't give himself away; he was a miserable liar in real life, unlike his persona, Lotus, who could tease and twist the truth.

Sahara ticked points off on his fingers. "The glass guy is fitting a window in your shop, the cleaning service you called is tidying up, and your friend Karen is watching over the whole operation so you can get a break. What's the big deal?" Sahara reached down, picked up his food, and took a bite out of his veggie wrap, looking cool and collected.

Seth glared at him, wishing he wasn't wearing smoke-tinted sunglasses which made it hard to read his expression, revealing only the occasional glimpse of fiery blue behind the shield of the lens.

He thought back over the blur of the very early morning. First, Sahara and Officer Martinez had really seemed chummy, depressing Seth even though he knew how stupid that was. The officer had often touched Sahara's hand or gripped his arm, very familiar for a cop; he'd definitely wanted to be on more intimate terms with Sahara.

Strangely, Sahara had seemed uncomfortable with the attention. At one point, when the rock and note were bagged and put away as evidence, he'd caught Seth's speculative look and actually blushed. Huh. Had he been embarrassed at the attentions of Martinez?

But it wasn't exactly something he could come out and ask Sahara.

While all this dancing had been going on between the two, Seth had gotten his act together. He'd weathered tough times before, having started doing trunk sales at craft shows all over the country before he could build up his online and storefront business. Now he shipped worldwide and also offered classes in a studio attached to his shop. Speaking of which, tonight was the next one, and Seth wasn't looking forward to it now, since he was drained.

As Sahara had just noted, he'd called the glass man and had a promise that by nine thirty a.m., when his shop opened on a Saturday, his glass would be replaced. Al, the guy he dealt with, fortunately had the dimensions needed on permanent record.

And then Karen had arrived, tall, brunette, and serene; she'd immediately given Sahara Blue an intense look before meeting Seth's eyes and raising a brow.

Seth had blushed, of course. He'd actually described his dream man to her once in a fit of beery moroseness, and now he knew his perceptive friend couldn't help but recognize him.

Karen had made it a point to introduce herself to Sahara.

"I want to take your boss out for breakfast," Sahara had told her abruptly, shocking Seth.

"That's a good idea," Karen agreed, amused brown eyes on Seth's surprised face. "No worries; I'll take care of things here."

And so they had walked down to the wharf just above where Sahara lived, and because Seth was a dolt and had forgotten his wallet, Sahara had treated him to a breakfast of hot coffee, refreshing watermelon juice, and a wrap.

"I REALLY need to change out of these clothes. I must be ripe by now," Sahara said, grimacing and shoving shaggy, sandy hair out of his eyes.

Seth blinked. Ripe? Sahara smelled good to him. Earthy. But he wisely kept the thought to himself, swallowing his disappointment that his time with Sahara was over. "Okay, I should get back to the shop."

"No. It's only eight. Why don't you come with me, spend some time?" Now Sahara looked a little uncomfortable. He was playing with the wrapping paper for his food, not looking up at Seth.

Seth's shoulders tensed. "No, um."

Sahara looked up. "You'd be doing me a favor!"

Seth hesitated. "Really?"

"Yeah, see, I was thinking…." Sahara blew out a breath and then pointed to a floating home at the pier below them. Not Sahara's place, Seth knew. "See that? That's my friends' Jared and Toby's house. It's… they have all this stuff, and it feels good to be there. I probably spend as much time at their digs as I can."

Seth wasn't sure where this was going, but he chewed his lip, listening. It was agonizing and scary and uplifting to be around Sahara Blue. And once he left here, he'd probably never see the guy again.

"But they are like newlyweds a lot of the time, you know? In fact, they only moved in together recently. So sometimes…." Sahara's voice drifted off. "Well, I feel more alone when I'm with them."

Seth's heart softened. It seemed maybe they had something in common. "My friend Karen is happily married. Always makes me wish…."

"So you understand," Sahara said. "But just this morning, before we met, I was thinking I'd like to try to find some of the things that, in Jared and Toby's house, make it so nice. Maybe then, when I'm alone in mine, I won't feel…."

Seth nodded. He liked to decorate his apartment, even if it was just for his own eyes. It did make him feel a little better about how alone he was. At least he had a space he enjoyed. "I understand. A lot of my single clients do just that."

"I knew you would." Sahara shrugged and then stood up, his body language still a little ill at ease, as if communicating his feelings didn't come easy to him.

Well, it wasn't easy for Seth, either, though he'd just assumed no one would ever want him. Certainly no one had ever shown much interest, not men or women. Except in his shop and on his blog, both places where Seth came out of hiding to pursue things he was passionate about.

SETH was hesitant to cross the threshold into Sahara's home, his world. Hands in the pockets of his shorts, he watched Sahara open the door and then step inside, the home rocking just slightly from their weight and footsteps. What would it be like to live here? It seemed like something Seth had dreamed of as a kid, like a magic carpet or a tree house.

As if reading Seth's wonder at his home, Sahara's face brightened, and he said, "I was having trouble sleeping where I was living. All the sounds… felt like a buzzing sound working over my skin." He swallowed. "Jared had a place down here, and when this one came up for sale, he suggested I buy it, so I did."

Seth wondered at the hint of some kind of rough time in Sahara's past, but though for a moment the normally vivid blue eyes were shadowed, he didn't share more, just stood with his hand on the open door, waiting on Seth.

"Hey, we have this strange tradition down here that when you invite someone inside your home, they come in," Sahara finally drawled.

Seth made a face. "Very funny." Heart beating, he stepped over the threshold and into Sahara's place. As he passed his host, some devil inside him made him prod, "Are you sure you know who you're inviting in your home?"

"Pretty sure you're not a creature of the night." Sahara looked unruffled... and slightly smug. He closed the door and leaned against it, muscular arms crossed. "I can handle *you*, little one."

"Yes, you can." The words were instinctive, true.

SAHARA'S place was barren, unremarkable. The great room, which included a galley kitchen and the living room, had a brown couch, a small brass table, and a TV set. Near the windows was the only intriguing piece of furniture, a hanging chair.

Shoulders hunched, Seth walked through the room, feeling a bachelor's vibe loud and clear while Sahara tracked him with his gaze. A place like this did not signal intimate nights with someone special.

"Hmmm?"

"Yeah, I can see it would be a tough contrast to someplace more... homey," Seth admitted.

Sahara's head fell back and he groaned, rubbing his neck. "I need help. But before that, I need a shower." Without giving Seth a second look, Sahara pulled off his T-shirt, revealing his California beach bum tanned and rippled torso, his small brown nipples.... By the time he reached the hallway, his shorts were also gone, showing off the high globes of his muscular ass and—

Seth inhaled sharply.

Sahara snapped a look over his shoulder. "Shit, forgot. My back."

Seth heard his own heartbeat ticking off the moment.

"Helo crash." Sahara's voice was absolutely flat. "Shrapnel, fire."

Seth's lips parted. His fingers curled, and he had to resist the urge to move closer to Sahara's tense body. Touch his pitted skin, traced by the seams of scars.

Sahara frowned. "I used to be pretty... unselfconscious about being naked, and for some reason with you I forgot about the scars. Guess you don't want to see them, fucking ugly, I know."

Moving in some kind of strange autopilot, Seth crossed the charged territory between him and Sahara. When he reached him, he fell to his knees and pressed his lips to Sahara's lower back.

Sahara made some kind of sound. He whirled around and lifted Seth easily, right off his feet. Then he set him down, and Seth swayed, shocky from his own bizarre actions and what he'd seen flare in Sahara's eyes.

"You're mine," Sahara said. "You may not know it. Better get used to it."

Seth stared blankly at him, and Sahara cursed before disappearing into his small bathroom, slamming the door behind him.

Still reeling from the moment, like being struck by hot, sizzling lightning out of the blue, Seth walked back to the couch and collapsed on top of it. Just what the hell had he unleashed?

SAHARA was in his bathroom a long time. The water ran and Seth fidgeted, wishing he could just leave. What would it matter if he did? Sahara couldn't have meant that strange vow. He'd just write Seth off as an odd, geeky guy he tried to take under his wing.

Yet the stuff brewing between them was like a thunderhead building. Seth didn't know what to make of it. He had no experience with a real relationship, other than his friendship with Karen. His foster parents had been as distant as cold planets when he'd been growing up, so even though he'd ached to connect with someone, he's spent most of his time alone. Karen he'd met through his dye business, since she'd loved his shop and returned often enough that they'd slowly become close friends. He'd been so needy for someone when she'd come along. Now he wasn't sure what he'd do without her.

Finally, unable to deal with the suspense of wondering when Sahara would appear again, Seth got up and wandered the great room, restless. He loved the view, of the other floating homes and little boats tied to the dock and of the harbor beyond. He bet Sahara spent a lot of time watching this living art. It was the most striking part of his home and maybe part of why, until recently, the other man hadn't been moved to decorate. What could compete with that? And yet if Sahara had experienced a home with warmth, it probably did make this place seem a little empty.

Curious to see if the other rooms were as sparse, Seth inched timidly toward an open door opposite the bathroom into what looked to be a small study. There was a battered wooden desk, like something you'd find Dumpster-diving, file folders and a shiny new state-of-the-art laptop, sitting closed. Nothing else in the room but a window offering another perspective of the harbor.

Seth's fingers brushed the file folders as he stared at the laptop and thought about how this was truly where he and Sahara Blue had met, not that he'd ever want the other man to know his secret. The gentle movement caused the papers to shift around, and one file folder flopped open, revealing an enhanced picture of a nude Seth, tied to a tree.

Seth's heart jumped in his throat.

Oh, shit, he remembered when he'd convinced Karen to take that. He'd been daydreaming, as usual, about meeting the kind of man who would find him sexy, about looking appealing for him in some sexy scenario, like the stories he made up and liked to share....

The bathroom door opened, shattering the moment, and steam escaped like dragon's breath into the study, heralding Sahara's arrival. Seth snapped the folder closed, swallowing tightly as Sahara peered inside the room, obviously looking for him.

"I... see what you mean about needing a few more things," Seth said, feeling more than ever like a mouse caught by a tiger. Why did Sahara have blown-up photographs from his blog? "You don't even have any art on the walls."

Sahara had a towel wrapped around his slim waist. His sandy hair was straight from the weight of water, pushed off his forehead and brushed back. He looked stern and handsome, like a statue in marble.

"I wouldn't know what to hang in here," he said, shaking his head. "My friends Jared and Toby seem to have a knack."

"I could help," Seth offered before he could stop himself. Oh, shit! What was he doing?

Sahara smiled. "Yes." Then he paused, and something that looked very much like shyness moved through his eyes. "I do make stuff sometimes."

Seth blinked at the change of topic. He was still wired from discovering that Sahara apparently was interested enough to blow up and store photographs of him in the nude—and would he somehow recognize Seth from those photos? Seth must make sure he wasn't naked around the other man, just in case, not that that would probably ever be a problem….

"Um?" He raised his brows, grateful to move out of the study and away from his high-octane discovery.

"Yeah." Sahara's voice was soft, husky. He nodded toward the last door in the hallway, which had to be to his bedroom.

Aware of a towel-wrapped Sahara on his heels, Seth peered in. There was a platform bed, plain and vaguely Japanese in style, and nothing else except windows and—

"*Wow!*" Despite himself, Seth moved deeper into the room, drawn to what swung gently from fishing wire strung across the windows in place of curtains. "Oh, man."

He touched one, purple feathers, beads in the most pleasing colors and arrangement, like a glittering, fantasy spider web. "Sahara."

Sahara was smiling faintly from in front of his closet as he pulled out worn jeans, white at the seams, and a blue T-shirt and plain black briefs. Seth couldn't look away when the other man dropped his towel, revealing a thick penis and the lusty, sandy hair surrounding it. Seth couldn't pretend to be casual about Sahara being nude. He was too beautiful to Seth's eyes.

"Your pendant," he croaked, seeking something else to focus on as Sahara pulled it over his head so it fell between his nipples, a flashing azure patch of beads. "You made it like you did all the dreamcatchers hanging at the window?"

Faint color touched Sahara's cheeks as he pulled on his briefs. He paused before tugging on jeans and nodded. "I do some beading. When I was in rehab, my fine motor control was funky, so I did shit to try to build it up. That's when I started making the dreamcatchers. Some dude taught a craft class, and I really liked them. And, you know, they are supposed to be helpful with your dreams." He looked at Seth under sandy brows. "I've never shown them to anyone before."

"But...." Hadn't he brought back men to his bedroom? Seth bet the hot Officer Martinez would love to get in here! Then he had a sudden idea. "You have to let me sell some in my shop."

Chapter Four

SAHARA opened his mouth, not sure what the fuck he was going to say, when he caught the sound of a hesitant knock on his front door, one that had a familiar quality.

"Come in, Toby!" he yelled to his friend.

Seth tensed at the abrupt summons. He guessed maybe it wasn't quite polite or something. He was constantly fucking up! He could still see the wide-eyed shock in Seth's eyes when he'd lifted him off his feet and declared his intentions. But how else could he react to such provocation? Seth had knelt for him, kissed him. Sealed his fate.

Sahara rubbed the back of his neck. He wished he could figure out what to say to Seth now. The man was very shy, and Sahara wanted desperately to kiss him, but he wasn't sure how to get near him.

"Sahara?" Jared called.

"I'm in my bedroom. With Seth." Sahara turned to face his two friends as he heard them stride down his hallway.

Jared and Toby peeked in, Toby looking amused for some reason. Sahara lifted a brow to signal his thought to his friend. *What are you looking at?*

"Are we interrupting, since you have a man, ah, in your bedroom?" Toby asked.

Sahara blinked, abruptly realizing how strange that must seem to his friends. He never brought his tricks back here.

"It's Seth," he said baldly, as if that said it all.

Jared's eyes sharpened on Seth, and Toby cocked his head before moving toward him and holding out his hand. Seth took it shyly, as if he couldn't resist Toby's natural puppy warmth.

Speaking of puppy…. "Where's Albert?" Sahara asked. He'd originally found their newly adopted puppy abandoned on the dock.

"Left him tied outside," Toby said, shrugging.

"He can come in."

"Are you sure? He's still having some training issues." Toby's eyes glinted ruefully. "I asked the vet when he'd have better control, and she said it would happen when his bladder grew large enough."

"What would I care?" Sahara asked, feeling deflated yet again by the barrenness of his space. "Look around you. My home is nothing special."

Jared frowned, brown eyes narrowed on Sahara, but Sahara shrugged off his other friend's intent look and instead focused on Seth, whose head was bent as he touched one of the dreamcatchers. He looked even more reserved than he had when they'd been alone. Fuck! Sahara wasn't exactly great at putting someone at ease at the best of times. He did all right in his job or with his friends, but whenever he thought someone was cute he turned into a useless asshole.

"You can have them all," he offered abruptly.

Seth shook his head, not looking pleased like Sahara had hoped. "Oh, I—"

"Look, I made them to…." He swallowed. He didn't think he wanted to admit aloud it was because he woke up a lot of nights and couldn't get back to sleep, too tense from the goddamned flashbacks. Way to look pathetic. "It'll save me tossing them out."

"No, don't do that!" Seth said, obviously distressed at the idea. He took a protective step closer to the hanging works, and then his face contorted and he grabbed his left leg, panting.

With instincts honed by combat, Sahara made it to Seth's side before he collapsed to the floor.

"Seth!" he barked, taking in the dilated pupils and the way Seth was gripping his leg, puffing, his face pale and sweating.

"What's wrong?" Jared asked, he and Toby also rushing to Seth's side. Seth's eyes rolled, and Sahara gestured them back.

"Some kind of reaction to stress," Sahara said absently. He nuzzled his forehead against Seth's. "Maybe a delayed reaction to something that happened earlier. Easy, baby. I've got you. Ease down...."

"M-my calf!" Seth rasped. "Charley horse. Shit! It's intense, Sahara!"

Sahara touched the skin of Seth's leg and found it drum-tight over knotted muscle. "It's okay. It's going to be absolutely fine." Sahara swung Seth into his arms, and the other man winced. Toby clutched Sahara's arm, empathy burning in his blue eyes.

"What can we do?"

"I'm taking him to the ER."

"What?" Toby's eyes rounded. Jared, however, fished out the keys to his beloved DeSoto and flipped them to Sahara, who didn't have wheels of his own when he wasn't working. "Just filled the tank. Toby and I will be right behind you."

"No, Sahara, it's just a charley horse," Seth said, his face flushed with embarrassment.

"It could be a lot more than that," Sahara chided. "Trust me."

As Sahara maneuvered swiftly from the room, Seth whispered, "I've seen your friends on TV, haven't I?"

"Yeah, they play lovers. Kind of worked into the real deal."

Seth's fingers clenched into Sahara's shoulders. His face was strained. "That's nice," he said.

SAHARA paced the waiting room of the ER, wishing he could smoke. He rarely got the urge he'd kicked when he'd decided to try out for the SEALs. As a candidate, he had to run, swim, and be in absolutely top shape, so he had stopped doing it when he'd trained for Hell Week.

"Hey," Jared said, gripping his shoulder. He was a quiet support, while Toby was more demonstrative, arm occasionally going around Sahara as if to let him know he wasn't alone.

"Just making sure he's okay," Sahara said, knowing his friends probably thought he'd overreacted, not that he gave a shit. This was Seth.

But just then, Seth finally appeared, still hobbling and looking self-conscious.

"It's not a blood clot," Seth whispered. "That's what you were afraid of, right?"

Sahara nodded. "I wasn't sure how active you are and... you seemed really tense at my house, dude."

Seth flushed. "It was just a stupid charley horse."

"Still hurts now, I bet," Sahara said. He was itching to carry Seth again, but he could see from his reserve that he wouldn't accept that. He took a deep breath, throttling back. "You aren't around people much?"

"I... um, not people like...." Seth nodded toward Jared and Toby. "Not famous."

Sahara wanted to laugh. His friends had pretend sex on a bad soap opera. But he could see now was not the time to tease Seth. Tenderness moved through him, something that felt strange but good.

"I'm taking you home."

"Good! Karen, my shop...."

"No, uh. *My* home."

Seth stared at him.

Sahara cleared his throat. "Look, your body had some kind of severe reaction to stress, like an allergy attack. You're hurting and you need someone to keep an eye on you. I called your shop, and Karen is going to look after it all day. She also canceled your class tonight."

"I'm all right." Seth frowned. "I'm a dweeb, but I can take care of myself."

"Seth, aren't you as important as your shop, as any class you might teach?" Sahara asked, very gently.

"I...." Seth blinked. "Yeah."

"Hmmm. Not the automatic answer I was looking for. So you'll stay the night at my place," Sahara stated, severe. Couldn't Seth see how special he was? Sahara would be happy to show him.

Seth's gaze flew to Jared and Toby, and Sahara shook his head. "It'll be just us. Unless I stress you out too."

"You... most of all," Seth admitted. His dark eyes were serious, and Sahara couldn't ignore that.

"I just want to take care of you like...." He swallowed. Damn. He guessed he had to lie since Seth was so reserved. "A friend."

Seth's shoulders relaxed minutely. "You're a very sweet person, but you don't need to do that."

"Hey, I'll heat up my hibachi and cook us some salmon steaks with a little salad. You can take it easy, and tomorrow morning you can go back to your shop, make sure it's shipshape for the coming week, okay?" And Sahara intended to go with him. He had to work the following evening, but he'd make sure Seth was okay before he did, and he'd drive by his place after he finished.

"I...." Seth chewed his lip. Then he gave Sahara a little smile. "I guess I could sleep on your couch. It's large enough."

"You'll take the bed," Sahara said.

SETH finally allowed Sahara Blue to put an arm around him and help him limp into a taxicab, since Sahara's friends had taken charge of their borrowed vehicle.

He was glad that Sahara had sent the gorgeous and intimidating men on their way. He knew he'd behaved like a complete loser, but he couldn't help that he'd never met any kind of celebrities before, and he'd watched *Mission Bay* since it had debuted. It was one of the few shows that depicted men like himself, even if the plot lines were silly sometimes and the romance a bit over the top. But the eye candy was smoking. How often had he drooled over Jared and Toby playing their characters?

It had been a hell of a shock when they'd walked into Sahara's home, and then… pain.

"Cut yourself some slack," Sahara said now, breaking into Seth castigating himself.

"How do you know what I'm thinking?" Seth asked, giving Sahara a grave look which the other man returned with an irreverent rise of a sandy eyebrow. His incredible blue eyes were amused but gentle on Seth's face.

"I know you, Seth," Sahara said, reaching for Seth's hand in the back of the taxi.

Seth flushed and jerked his hand away.

Sahara settled back with a sigh. "Okay," he said.

"Okay what?" Seth wasn't sure what was going through the blond's mind. He didn't know if he trusted that sudden serene look.

"Okay, we do it your way until we can do it mine," Sahara said as they pulled up at the wharf.

When they got out of the vehicle, Sahara got the fare but Seth insisted he would cover it later. Sahara shrugged, though Seth sensed he had to think about it first. He wanted to roll his eyes at how protective the other man seemed. Seth could take care of himself, despite how pathetically he'd behaved earlier. He wanted to make that very clear to Sahara Blue.

"I asked Karen to drop by around dinnertime to give you an update on the shop."

Seth blinked, hobbling next to Sahara since his calf was still knotted, the muscles spasming at unpredictable intervals, though thankfully not as badly as earlier. "Thanks, that will make me feel a lot better."

"She's also bringing you a few things for spending the night with me."

Seth insisted, "I'm not. Spending the night with you, I mean. I'm just...." He wasn't sure what. How had Sahara ordered him into doing this? But it was like that weird moment when he'd knelt behind the bigger man, touching his scarred flesh with his lips. Seth had felt something shift between them, felt like he had done something that could not be undone.

"Sure, little one," Sahara said, smiling enigmatically.

Abruptly irritated, Seth snapped, "Don't call me that."

"But you like it," Sahara contradicted.

Seth did. He growled softly to himself.

Sahara smiled.

SAHARA left Seth at his place, taking it easy on his couch with the TV remote close at hand. He had to get some dinner for the two of them to barbeque, and he needed some tips on polishing his act—in a hurry. He pounded on Jared and Toby's door, hoping he wasn't interrupting them. But if he was, they just wouldn't answer, he figured.

The door opened, and a smug-looking Toby grinned at him. "You have a boyfriend."

"Cut it out!" Sahara said, though he could feel himself coloring. Toby always sliced through the bullshit.

"Come on, the way you're acting? It's the way Jared behaves with me," Toby noted.

"Is he here?"

Toby shook his head. "He was scheduled to tape a promo spot for the show, so he's off doing that for a while. What do you need?" The shorter blond crossed his arms, and Sahara looked beyond him to the beautiful home he'd made with his lover and partner.

Sahara sighed, wishing for just a little of that ambiance. He wanted to make things special for Seth.

"I need help choosing some food, and I want something for my bedroom."

Toby covered what looked suspiciously like a smile with his palm.

"Not toys!" Sahara growled. "Just… something Seth might like. Have you seen his shop? It's that dye joint a few blocks up from here."

Toby nodded. "Jared and I have gone there sometimes to buy cloth for pillows. It's a beautiful place, though we've always visited on our free Mondays when a woman is working, so I don't remember meeting Seth before today."

Sahara relaxed slightly. Toby might tease, but he had the sense he understood Seth was special to him. "So will you help me?"

"Sure, it's time Albert goes for a walk anyway," Toby said, snagging his wallet and picking up a leash for the puppy before snapping it on the little dog. "Maybe fresh fish and veggies for dinner, which you can get when we return to the wharf market, but I'd suggest something from the Italian bakery for dessert."

"Yeah?" Sahara asked. He watched and approved as Toby set the new alarm and locked the floating home up securely. He never wanted his friends devastated by another home invasion again. "I was thinking salmon steaks."

"Sounds good. You could also get some cannoli rolls, or…." Toby and Albert set off, keeping up with Sahara's long strides as they walked up the pier. "They have burnt butter tarts."

"I want something special for Seth. Maybe… a cake. Is that too much?"

"I don't think so. What do you want for the bedroom?"

Sahara sighed. "I don't know. Something. I guess I'll know it when I see it."

"I'll try to pretend I have Jared's sensibilities," Toby said, rueful. "Your Seth is okay, isn't he? I think Jared and I freaked him out. Did you tell him I clean pools as my regular job?"

"What I think is, he's a virgin," Sahara said flatly. "But I'll take care of that."

SAHARA lucked out in finding the special something in the garden shop located next to the Italian bakery. First, he bought a fluffy cake, tiramisu, the topping a caramel color that looked lush and inviting. He couldn't help it if he pictured breaking off pieces of the cake and anointing Seth's nipples and sucking and licking them from his slight body.

Sahara wanted to mount the other man, crush him into the bed. But he supposed he had better be good and behave, given how timid Seth seemed. He'd been shaken up that day, and Sahara had hated to see him in pain. He wanted him flushed and satisfied and relaxed.

After securing dessert, they'd paused outside the garden shop, and Sahara's eye had been caught. Without a clue what it was or why he thought *Seth*, he pointed toward it. "That," he said.

Toby gave another little smile, half amused, half hopeful. It was obvious he wanted to see something happen for his friend. "A Balinese goddess?"

"Is that what it is?" They entered the shop, and the clerk brought them the blond limestone piece, something like a slab with a serene face carved into it. It reminded Sahara a little of a statue Jared had of Kwan Yin, goddess of mercy.

Sahara paid for it and hefted it without complaint, though it wasn't light. But tonight Seth would sleep beside it. Tonight his bedroom wouldn't be so barren.

And if he could find a way to work it, he'd sleep with Seth.

Chapter Five

"MY GOODNESS!" Seth exclaimed when Sahara returned, feeling like a hunter who was loaded down with spoils. The Balinese goddess banged against his leg as he unloaded his supplies; he left her wrapped and on the bed for now, as a surprise for Seth later—the man was sure to notice the new touch in Sahara's empty space. Would he guess the reason why Sahara had made the effort?

"Yeah," he said, smiling as he returned to the galley kitchen to place the salmon steaks in the sink and the ready-made Greek salad on the counter. It was close to dinnertime, so he'd go and fire up the old-fashioned coals to get them to the white-hot temperature best for cooking.

"I thought this was a just a friend thing," Seth said, getting up with apparent stiffness and limping over for a closer look at Sahara's purchases. "I mean… cake."

Sahara's chest tightened at these signs of discomfort, but he guessed he was overreacting a little. Yet from the moment he'd first looked at Seth, huddled in the dark of his shop with broken glass between them, he'd wanted to take care of the man.

"I have very friendly feelings," Sahara deflected, watching as Seth eyed the cake. "And I love tiramisu."

"So do I. What's not to love? Italian. Cream. And those little cookies soaked in amaretto."

Sahara smirked. "Exactly."

"But tiramisu seems a boyfriend thing."

"Have you ever had one?" Sahara decided to push Seth so he'd stop fussing.

"No." Seth flushed. "It's just... cake."

"Cake is definitely a serious commitment," Sahara admitted. "To be friends. Come here...." He pulled Seth into his arms and felt the tension there begin to ease as he rubbed the slighter man's back. "Seth," he whispered. His throat closed since he didn't know what else to say. He was afraid of fucking things up. Seth was clearly suspicious he was being romanced, and Sahara didn't want to put him in the hospital from another anxiety attack.

Sahara took a deep breath, looking at Seth, his long, dark eyelashes, his pale skin, his slanted brown eyes and curly hair. What was it about him that got to Sahara, turned him on? "I'll fire up the barbeque."

"I'll help out," Seth said, stubborn to the last.

Sahara wanted to growl at him to lie down and take it easy. Instead he nodded, giving in. He could give Seth a little rope. For now.

KAREN showed a few minutes after Sahara started up his hibachi, lighting the coals. She was wide-eyed as she climbed from the pier to Sahara's floating home and then up the metal ladder to the rooftop.

"Wow," she whispered to Seth, squeezing his shoulder. "You okay? I heard about the leg."

"Yeah." Seth didn't want to talk about how useless he'd been. At least Sahara was occupied with the food, so he got to watch the beautiful man and enjoy the view. It was easier than being the focus of those vivid blue eyes.

"I've never known anyone who lived in one of these. It's like a grown-up tree house," Karen marveled.

Seth looked around at the dancing sunlit water and the busy activity on the wharf and the sailing and power boats coming in. It was a lively place, nothing like his quiet rooms above the shop where he often lay on his bed and heard the loud tick of his old-fashioned grandfather clock.

"It is magical," Seth agreed, gaze riveted on Sahara Blue. His hair was ruffled from the sea breeze, and there was fine sandy stubble on his jaw and cheeks. He was wearing the smoky sunglasses again, and yet every now and then, a beam of intense blue shot in Seth's direction, making him catch his breath.

"Tiramisu…," Karen said.

"Don't start!" Seth put up a finger, hoping to head his friend off.

"Come on. He has to be interested, because… well, *cake*."

"I did mention to him that I thought it was an extravagance."

"And?" Karen took a sip of the white wine Sahara had offered her, unruffled when she'd shown up, as if he and Seth were just friends… or an established couple.

"And he seems to want to spoil me." Seth cursed his pale skin, since he knew that the blush had to be touching the tips of his ears.

"I'd say it's about time, so let him." Karen reached out and gripped Seth's hand. "Oh, Seth, just let someone get close, please."

"I have my shop, my friends…." He didn't include the blog, since she often scolded him about his assumption that he was building connections online that weren't real, that a lot of it was in his head. He sighed. Well, she was partly right, but his crush on Sahara Blue had turned out to be all too real.

"That's not enough for a romantic heart," Karen whispered.

"Karen!" Seth shook his head at her sappiness, even though her description felt oddly right. Not that he'd ever admit it aloud. He was a guy, after all.

Sahara Blue interrupted their confidences by offering them plates of steaming food, including Karen, who looked startled but then delighted. "Eat up," he said. "Save some room for cake."

Karen smiled. "Oh, I'll let you boys have your cake without me."

Sahara lowered his sunglasses and quirked a brow at Karen.

"SO IF this were your place, what would you do to make it more homey?" Sahara asked casually after Karen waved and headed down the pier.

Feeling wildly conscious of the fact that he was alone with Sahara again, Seth was glad for the slice of cake placed in front of him on the coffee table. It gave him something to do with his hands as he watched Sahara fiddle around in his kitchen, pulling out spices, bottled whipped cream—and didn't his mind go somewhere that he hoped wasn't too obvious on seeing that can! Yet from the amused look Sahara directed at him, no doubt taking in the color that stung Seth's cheeks, he figured Sahara guessed.

"There. Monte Cristo coffees," Sahara said triumphantly, returning to the couch to sit next to Seth.

Seth lifted his mug, sniffing the delicious aroma. "I haven't had one of these in years!"

"I don't think they are as popular now, but I love them. Very indulgent," Sahara said, sipping from his own mug. He fell back lazily against his couch, looking satisfied at the meal he'd provided. "Sometimes after diving somewhere really freaking cold, I'd get a yen for one of these. Couldn't indulge on duty, though."

Seth dared to study him openly, sipping his own drink, which burned with a tang of sweetness. Sahara's sandy hair was tangled around his face, his stubble outlining full lips; lips that Seth imagined were a hundred times more experienced than his own. He could easily picture the other man kissing someone… or sucking his cock.

The last thought sent a *zing* to Seth's cock, so he shifted uncomfortably.

"I think that you should take it slow," he said, glad for the distraction of decorating Sahara's home. "Find things that speak to you, listen to how you feel about them. If you think of it, your friend Jared probably did that at first when he was learning to create his home."

Sahara's brows rose. "So it's just like a muscle you work in training?"

"Yes, I don't see why it's any different. Some people do have particular talents for things, but with some time and attention, I think you can build something you are happy with."

Sahara's blue eyes gleamed at him over his foamy mug. "I would need help. Like someone spotting me at the gym."

"I'm sure you can find someone."

"I already have," Sahara said, raising an eyebrow.

"I don't know." Seth shifted around on his seat again. "Perhaps I was impulsive before, offering my services."

"You haven't eaten any cake yet," Sahara scolded, ignoring Seth's comment. He sat up, T-shirt bunching over rippling muscle, far more enticing than any dessert, and took hold of Seth's fork. "Open for me, Seth," he purred.

A flash of heat brought color to Seth's face and neck, made his nipples harden as he held Sahara's brilliant blue eyes. He opened his mouth, and Sahara placed the treat on his tongue. Seth squeezed his eyes shut and moaned at the taste. "Ohhhh."

"You'll like everything I put in your mouth," Sahara said.

"You're a tease!" Seth said with a laugh, shoving aside the fork, but Sahara persisted with more cake, making it clear he intended to feed his guest.

"I am not. A tease." Blue eyes burned him, but Seth wanted to be burned, so he ate the cake, savoring the rich dessert and holding Sahara's gaze as he did so. It was such a sexy scenario, it reminded him of the stories he wrote on his blog sometimes, and he had a guilty desire to compose something, like a bit of music in his head.

But Sahara had no idea who he was, about his double life. How could he reveal the deception now? With every hour it became more impossible. Somehow, even though it seemed, incredibly, as if Sahara was bent on becoming friends with him, Seth would have to keep his secret.

Sahara's BlackBerry buzzed, and he cursed, putting down the fork. He pulled it out of the pocket of his shorts and read the message. "Have to cover for someone for an hour. Fuck!"

"Don't worry," Seth said, reaching out and cupping a hand around Sahara's wrist. "I'll be fine. I can still go home...."

"*No.*" Sahara took a deep breath, as if aware he sounded a little over the edge. "I, uh, really want to be sure you're okay. Can you stay as a favor to me?"

Seth saw sincerity in the remarkable blue eyes. "Of course," he said, unable to deny his new friend anything.

"Thanks," Sahara said, giving a rueful shrug before he disappeared down the hallway at a jog.

IT WAS only two minutes after Sahara left, dressed in a black silk suit, smoky sunglasses, slicked back hair, gun strapped on under his jacket and his signature pendant, that Seth found himself drawn again to Sahara's study.

He stared at the laptop sitting on the battered desk, feeling the impulse to get online and purge himself of some of his chaotic feelings in one of Lotus's bedtime stories.

He'll never know, Seth comforted himself before booting up the powerful computer and logging on. Just out of curiosity, he used "My Favorites" in the browser, and number one was Lotus's site. So Sahara was definitely as fixed on shy Seth's alter ego as Seth had been focused on him.

Closing his eyes, he let all that go and just spilled himself in tapping keys.

HOURS later, Sahara sighed wearily as he climbed onto the deck surrounding his floating home. An hour. Shit. It had turned into nearly seven. He could see that his house was dark now. Had Seth taken off? It was too much to hope he'd kept his promise and waited for Sahara when he'd ended up delayed so long.

Disappointment rode him as he quietly unlocked the door, but still a little hope tugged, like a kite that wanted to get off the ground, fly. Sahara's heart was beating hard as he removed his jacket and the holster for his weapon. The floor creaked under his dress shoes as he ghosted to his bedroom door, pushed it open gently.

Seth was lying in a pool of moonlight, lips parted, eyes closed, dark brows and eyelashes giving him a serene look. He was modestly wearing a T-shirt and boxers, having pushed the duvet down the bed.

Gut tight, Sahara continued into his room, removing his formal clothing until he wore only his own boxers and the pendant he'd made for himself. Giving in to his need, he knelt by the bed and stroked the hair off Seth's forehead. The other man didn't wake from the tiny caress.

Sahara sat back on his heels, spotting the plastic and paper-wrapped package by the bed. He'd forgotten about it in his hurry to get to work. Careful not to disturb Seth, he unwrapped the Balinese goddess and then stood her next to him, on the bare hardwood floor, since Sahara lacked even a bedside table.

HE GAVE in to one last nagging impulse and stole into his study, logging on. He felt vaguely guilty for still being intrigued by sexy Lotus when he had shy Seth in his bed, but he'd been reading the man for months and this was the longest he'd gone without checking in.

His breath caught in his throat, and sweat popped out on his forehead when he saw that Lotus had posted another one of his stories about the boy enslaved in a cage on a futuristic world.

For months, my master did not touch me except to bathe me and to keep me close for company. I began to be grateful for and seek out his caresses, since it made me feel less lonely, but I needed sex, and of course I fixated on the barbarian with his silky pelt and loin cloth. But how to make him take me?

I decided drastic measures were required, and although I was frightened of being punished—he had never really done it, but that didn't mean he wouldn't—I decided I needed to provoke him.

The next evening when he opened my cage, expecting me to go obediently to my bath so he could wash me with a cloth, running his big hands all over me, instead I made a break for it, as if I meant to escape his cozy den!

I'd made it maybe seven paces when he tackled me and I fell face down on the soft rug next to his chair. I could feel his heart thudding; felt the way he gripped me, hard enough to leave bruises. Oh, yes, I had his attention.

But what most interested me was the prod of his hard penis against my backside. Surely now he would—

He yanked me over his lap and swatted my ass. It was not a pleasant spanking; it hurt. I put my hand over my backside to protect myself, but my cock was hard, and I knew he had to feel it.

Fed up that this would be another futile exercise and I wouldn't get what I wanted from him, I squirmed as if I was trying to get free. I was rewarded with another whack, and then he shoved me onto the rug, raised my ass—

I wasn't ready for his penetration, so my rough sound as he tried to push inside wasn't feigned discomfort. He panted above me, hand clenched around the back of my neck. I knew he hadn't planned to take me, knew I'd driven him to this.

He pulled out, and I made a sound of disappointment, lying there, limp, with my ass burning, but a moment later he'd returned, and I felt cool, oily fingers push inside me.

My owner wanted to prepare me for his use.

Eager slut that I was for him, I pushed back, riding his fingers. He stroked my prostate lightly, and I arched my back.

He mounted me again, and I spread myself. I was rewarded this time by the slick hand reaching in front of me and fisting my cock.

He pressed inside slower this time, making growling-pleasure sounds. His penis was long and thick, and it took time for me to accommodate him.

I expected him to ride me hard after my game, but he was ruthless, in control. He thrust slow and evenly, tapping against my gland. When I trembled and tried to get more sensation, he kept me immobile, and when I came close to coming, he stopped. When it happened a third time, I realized my owner was not going to allow me to come; that was to be my real punishment for trying to play him.

I accepted it, desperate to be fucked, and held still for him. He rutted for a long time, and I caught a glimpse of his reflection on the shiny rock surface of the wall beyond, eyes half closed, almost feline enjoyment.

Finally he spurted in me, biting the back of my neck as he came, but his hand was wrapped around my cock firmly, denying my release.

When he was done, he bathed me the same as always, ignoring my needy penis. Later, when he used me as a footstool, I nuzzled his foot. I wanted his attentions inside me again, but now I was finding a better way to ask him.

He seemed to approve, because he combed his fingers through my hair.

Sahara paced his study after he shut off his laptop. Jesus! He wasn't sure he could sleep now with his raging hard-on.

He walked out into the hallway and looked in at innocently sleeping Seth. Finally, hesitantly, he went to the bed, pulled back the duvet, and climbed in with him.

SETH heard Sahara Blue return in the early morning hours but feigned sleep, unsure of how to handle being in the alluring man's bed, especially after he'd excited himself so much by what he'd written as Lotus.

He heard the crinkle of Sahara unwrapping the mystery package he'd noticed earlier, and when the man disappeared, Seth sat up to take a look. In the moonlight, he made out the serene face of an Asian statue, he thought maybe Balinese. He touched the blond stone in wonder. Why did he think there was some significance connected to himself in Sahara having the piece? He shook his head. He had to be off.

When he heard Sahara return a short time later, he snapped his eyes closed from pondering the carving in the semi-darkness. Finally, Sahara stopped his restless pacing and got into the bed with Seth. Seth lay rigid, unsure of what to do. He'd never slept with another person in his life.

Sahara shifted closer, and Seth felt his hand stroke his bottom. A moment later, Sahara tugged down the material of his boxers, and then Seth felt a hard penis rub against him. Sahara gave a pained sound and then thrust against Seth, hand gripping his hip gently.

Warm liquid spurted on Seth's ass, and Sahara still held him, trembling, breathing hard. "Seth," he whispered, licking Seth's neck as if he needed to taste him.

Heart thudding, Seth waited to see what else Sahara would do. His cock ached, unsatisfied, desperate for a touch, but he was pretending to be asleep....

Sahara leaned away and the bed creaked, and then cool cotton—Sahara's T-shirt?—rubbed away the wetness on Seth's body. Another moment, and the larger man sighed softly and spooned Seth from behind. One long, muscled arm moved around Seth, taking possession.

Hungry for sex, still feeling Sahara's come on his body, Seth eventually calmed, staring out the window at the dark sea and lights of the harbor beyond.

Chapter Six

SETH had showered in a hurry when he'd woken to discover the impression of a body beside him on the low, Japanese-style bed but no sign of Sahara Blue. It was a relief after what he'd experienced the night before. Why had Sahara worked himself off against him? Seth would have thought it just a nightly ritual, making use of any warm body, but he could still hear Sahara's thready voice uttering, "*Seth.*"

Obviously Sahara had been thinking of him.

He donned the fresh boxers that Karen had thoughtfully brought over—and whoa, she'd loaded him down with a *lot* of clothing—for heaven's sake, did she think he'd be moving in with Sahara?

He took a deep breath, looking out at the view while his fingers grazed the top of Sahara's new Balinese statue. He'd wanted to ask him about it, but when he'd woken up, exhausted from being too tense to sleep most of the night, the other man had been gone.

The front door to the floating home slammed, and it swayed slightly, reminding Seth of how he'd spent the night in such an unusual place—hardly grounded, in more ways than one. He couldn't allow himself to have expectations about what he'd experienced with Sahara; the man was only in his life because of an accident.

"Seth," Sahara called, in much the same tone he'd used the night before when he'd marked Seth with his come.

Seth blushed at that thought.

"I bought breakfast." Sahara held up a paper bag as he entered the bedroom. "Veggie wraps from the wharf stands. And some hot coffee from Starbucks since my own machine was acting cranky today."

Seth's lips quirked as he remembered how hard Sahara had worked it to create special Monte Cristo coffees. "Maybe it's played out after last night?"

"Maybe." Sahara looked rueful. "I bought it ten years ago. Think it's time for a change?"

"Yep." Seth's eyes warmed, and for a moment he forgot he was standing there, his slender, pale chest revealed. Since his lack of muscle embarrassed him, especially around Sahara, he quickly snagged a T-shirt.

Sahara spread the food out on the bed, and after hesitating over this intimate setting, Seth timidly joined him, taking a hot wrap and some sour cream from Sahara's hand.

"This is how I start most of my days," Sahara said, shrugging. "I'd love to learn how to cook and shit, but...."

"It's always going to be another day." Seth nodded, recognizing the wishful thinking he also indulged in. "I feel that way about, you know, getting in shape."

Sahara stirred his coffee with a wooden stick, looking under his sandy brows at Seth in surprise. "You seem in good shape to me."

"I mean... you know, built up."

Sahara blinked. "Oh, yeah." He frowned. "The guys I'm usually with...."

"Are usually like you, right? All muscle." Seth's lips tugged down.

"But I've never brought any of them home," Sahara countered. "Well, I think I need to learn to cook more than you need to work out. You look...." He swallowed, and Seth knew he could probably see clearly how vulnerable Seth was feeling before he looked away. "I like how you're, uh, shaped. Nice."

"Yeah, sure."

Sahara reached out and gripped Seth's wrist. "Hey."

"Look, you don't have to just say things like that, okay?" Seth burst out, feeling regret riding him a second too late. His discomfort with his body had to be in neon. Terrific.

"Seth, put down your food," Sahara said in a conversational tone.

Seth blinked. "What?"

Sahara gently took the roll from Seth's grasp. "Stand up."

"Why?"

"Because I said so."

Seth stood. Then he flushed a deep red because he had responded to Sahara on a level that he'd never lived as Seth, but only as Lotus. What was happening?

Sahara wiped his hands and then came unhurriedly to his feet. His longish hair was pulled back in a ponytail, and he was still wearing the smoky sunglasses from being outside in the bright morning sunlight. He was unshaven, his hard, muscular body gloved by black jeans and a tank top.

If Lotus were writing about him, he'd describe this look as killer and dream up a scenario where he was some hot, dangerous man, some kind of special ops figure who was watching over Seth. And come to think of it, given Sahara's background, that wasn't far from the truth.

Seth had been distracted by his wandering thoughts, so he gasped when Sahara was suddenly looming close, a head taller, looking down at Seth expressionlessly.

"Seth...."

Sahara's hand reached out, confident, and cupped Seth intimately, weighing his cock and balls in his palm.

Seth gave a sharp sound, heart jumping. He stepped away, shifting back into the corner of Sahara's bedroom.

He stared into Sahara's eyes, expecting... what? Holy shit, they were in a world beyond anything he'd ever experienced except in fantasy! Panting, he waited for Sahara to speak, to apologize or skate over the primal moment.

But when Sahara finally said something, his words surprised Seth. "Do I repulse you?"

"*No!*" Bald, instinctive, the truth sizzled between them. "You're... I like you."

Sahara stepped closer again, eyes hidden behind lenses, face cool. He reached out, easy and deliberate, and took Seth's sex into his possession again.

And Seth sagged against the corner of the room, head falling back, lips parting. There was no sound in the room except the thunder of his heart as Sahara stroked him, slow, exploring him through the thin cotton of his boxers.

Seth gave a choked sound as his cock stiffened, helpless under that touch to do anything else. He could hear the rasp of Sahara's callused fingertips against the nap of his underwear.

"This is beautiful," Sahara said. He squeezed Seth very gently so there was no mistaking what he meant. "I want this."

Seth trembled. He thought his legs might give out, only he needed to be petted, stroked, so he stayed exactly how he was, braced, letting Sahara touch him as he liked.

"Seth, is this mine?" Sahara asked in an absorbed tone as his index finger ran down the length of Seth's hard penis.

Seth had to clear his throat twice. He couldn't meet Sahara's eyes. His gaze had fallen to the side, fixed on the base of the window, on the reflection of the glittering water. "Yes."

And Sahara scolded softly, "I can't hear you."

"Yes, it's yours." Now he looked at Sahara, knowing that his vulnerability, the moisture in his eyes, had to be fully evident.

Sahara's mouth firmed. "You didn't get to come last night."

"What?" Seth gaped at Sahara.

"Because you were busy pretending you were asleep when I rubbed myself off on your ass," Sahara noted. One sandy brow arched above the cool reflection of tinted glass. "Oh, you didn't think I believed you were asleep, did you?"

"I... guess not." Seth hadn't fooled Sahara! Would he ever be able to pull anything that the other man didn't somehow find out? The thought made his secret shift uneasy in his gut. "Why did you do it?"

"I wanted my come on you," Sahara admitted, very simply. "Don't faint. I don't want to take you back to the ER."

"I don't want to go back there again, either!" Seth snapped.

Sahara only smiled at this sudden show of spirit. "Isn't this better?"

The cloth was saturated where the tip of his penis had bloomed fluid. He could imagine how he looked, leaning against the wall in Sahara's shadowed bedroom, body tight as wire, hips thrust out, cock wanton, like a pet pleading for touch....

"Yes, it's better," he whispered.

"I knew you'd see things my way sooner or later, Seth," Sahara said, very gently. He loomed closer now so that he boxed Seth in. Their eyes clashed and locked as Sahara rubbed Seth's prick up and down through the cool cloth.

"Uh! Sahara!" Seth reached up and grabbed the other man's arms, not to stop him, but to keep him in place. He never wanted this to end, but it was unbearable. He was so hard.

"No one's ever touched you like this," Sahara observed, sounding smug. "No one's ever brought you off before."

"No one," Seth repeated. Sahara was toying with him now. Bringing him close to the threshold, right over the flame, and then softly pulling back. A rub to the top of his swollen tip and he gasped, eyes brimming with tears. It was too much.

"Spread your legs for me, Seth."

Seth obeyed, living for sensation now.

Sahara knelt in one graceful motion and put warm lips to the sensitive underside of Seth's balls.

"*Christ!*" His hands caged Sahara's head, feeling silky hair against his agitated fingers. "Please, Sahara, please...."

"Suck it?"

"God, yes!"

Sahara didn't take away the cloth, which made it seem even sexier, more illicit somehow. Instead he put his open mouth against the stem of Seth's cock, and Seth gave another grunt.

Sahara tugged down his boxers, but not in front where the maneuver only made the cloth pull tighter around Seth's wildly sensitized penis. Instead, he revealed the upper moons of Seth's ass, so he could feel cooler air and then a smooth, tracing finger moving down his body to rub against his opening.

"Ah!" Seth felt like one of the *ukes* in the *yaoi* manga he liked to read. Sahara definitely fit the role of the ruthless top, or *seme*, making Seth experience desire.

"No one's ever touched you here, virgin." Sahara's voice was drowsy now, as if he, too, were caught up. Seth could see perspiration dotting his upper lip, and his sunglasses were slightly askew as he brought his big body into contact with Seth's shaking one. His penis was a hot, hard imprint against Seth's body.

"No, no one but you, Sahara," Seth confessed poignantly. "I...." He didn't know what he was going to say, something insane, probably, but then the tip of Sahara's finger penetrated him and it was too much.

Seth spilled hotly, head arching back, Sahara's captive.

Chapter Seven

SETH had no idea what he would have said after Sahara worked him off. Made a joke that he might wind up in the ER again? He was shaking, legs giving out, and then Sahara swept him up in his arms, nuzzling his neck with parted lips so Seth could feel the warmth of the other man's breath against his chilled skin.

"Sahara." He gripped Sahara's arms.

"Shit," Sahara muttered. "Shit, I got… carried away. Don't freak, Seth."

Seth stared at Sahara.

"I know you're a very shy person. Don't hide under a rock, okay?" Sahara shoved open his bathroom door with one brawny shoulder and then lowered Seth carefully to his feet. "You need another shower."

Seth flushed, embarrassed. His boxers were sticking to him.

"Do you have fresh underwear?" Sahara was all business, removing his sunglasses and crossing his arms so Seth could feel the full effect of his concerned blue eyes.

"Yes. Karen bought far too much. I think she thought I'd be staying with you for days or something!" Seth said.

"No, I told her to do that," Sahara admitted absently.

Seth's eyes widened. "But…."

"You okay to, um, shower alone?"

Seth's head fell forward. He avoided Sahara's gaze. "Yes."

"Okay, then." Sahara sounded disappointed. "The laundry is opposite the bathroom when you get out. Just chuck in your shorts when you're done, and I'll start a wash." He paused, licking his lips. "Enjoy your shower, Seth."

UNDER the hot water spray, Seth reached down and touched himself, finding his penis already semi-erect. Had he been wrong in thinking that Sahara had wanted him to invite him into the shower with him? What then would have happened?

He flushed, as he had an idea that it would not be his hand on his cock now, but Sahara's.

He gave a thready moan at the thought.

Never before had he felt like *that*. Sahara had lifted him out of his rut of a life. It was as if the other man was Superman and had taken him flying. How did you come back to earth?

HE FOUND a fresh towel and a T-shirt and underwear sitting folded neatly on the cabinet by the sink. His throat tightened a little at the invisible care. He felt like Belle in his favorite Disney movie, *Beauty and the Beast*, when the servants take care of her.

Sahara had left him alone to shower, not pushing, and now he'd left Seth some clothing so that he wouldn't have to come out wearing only a towel, which would have left Seth feeling very much at a disadvantage. He still didn't understand why Sahara was behaving the way he was. He couldn't really want Seth?

SAHARA forced himself to be cool, though he paced his bedroom, rubbing his hair until it was in messy peaks and half out of its neat ponytail.

How was it one slight man had turned his life upside down? It was like Sahara had navigated one course, and then there was Seth and now he felt like he'd run his sailboat aground on an islet.

He had been trying to be so good, so careful. Seth was so timid he'd figured on a strategy of slow romance. Maybe when he got him a little more relaxed, they could get to the good part, to Sahara getting on top of him. But he'd found he enjoyed making special coffee for him and breathing in the scent of his hair in Sahara's formerly lonely bed.

It sure as shit was better than walking around with an aching prick and emptiness in his gut. Even Lotus's provocative stories didn't satisfy him, since there was no one to touch him, no one to talk to. He wanted what Jared had; someone to take care of, someone to spoil and make love to. He shook his head at his own romantic leanings.

But now he pursed his lips, beaded pendant sliding against his skin as he tried to think what next, what to do to keep Seth with him? Huh. He didn't like the idea of Seth going home to his shop and then Sahara having to sleep here alone tonight.

There had to be something….

His eyes widened as he hit on an obvious ploy.

"FIX your place?" Seth said, nibbling on his lip. "What, now?"

Sahara wanted to kiss that lip but managed to shove down his more aggressive tendencies. Crap. What must Seth think of how he'd taken "charge" of him previously? He couldn't tell, except he guessed it was a good thing his houseguest hadn't run in the other direction.

Now Seth looked particularly hot to Sahara in a blue long-sleeved T-shirt and jeans. He was wearing leather sandals, and his brown hair fell softly around his face, lightly curled from his shower.

Sahara's cock ached with the need to mount Seth on his bed and rub himself against him, but he wanted Seth to stay and that was hardly likely to do it. He had to do his reconnaissance. Study his prey.

"Yeah, starting with my bedroom," Sahara said. He shrugged. "Look, I told you I was unhappy with my place, that it feels... uh, kind of empty. Think of this as a decorating emergency."

Seth nodded solemnly, although his eyes twinkled at Sahara's last statement. Maybe he was laying it on a bit thick, but at least Seth was listening.

"The truth is, Seth...." Sahara took a deep breath, because this wasn't easy for him. Even before he'd been a big, bad SEAL and then gone through hell to recover and build a new life, he'd hated to be vulnerable to anyone. But it was different with Seth. "You being here last night was the first time anyone's stayed over, other than Jared and Toby."

Seth blinked.

"Um, no, I'm not involved with them." Shit. How was he going to explain that sometimes he played with them, very mildly? Though less and less as time went on. It wasn't a boyfriend thing. "I'm alone, Seth," he finished, and then thought, *Wow, I sound like a loser. Way to win him over. I should just make some shit up. Why can't I do that?*

Seth swallowed, staring into Sahara's eyes as if just seeing him. "What about other guys? I mean, looking the way you do...."

"I sometimes go somewhere, have some quick relief in an alley," Sahara confessed. "But I don't like anyone touching my back."

"I touched your back."

"That was *you*."

"Oh." Seth didn't look like he knew what to make of Sahara's statement.

"Yeah, so I really need your help." Sahara hated to ask for it, yet maybe it wasn't so different from the teamwork he'd been part of on the teams. From the beginning, SEALs buddied up. He'd just have to do that with Seth, kind of.

"I guess so." Seth looked around the bedroom and then gave a shy smile. "At least you don't have too much stuff, so you can make a fresh start."

"Yeah, except I want to keep the Bali lady. She's… nice, you know?"

Seth nodded, touching the blond stone carving. "I really like her, she's a great find. Did you get her at that garden shop next to the bakery with the tiramisu?"

"I have no secrets," Sahara said, smiling at Seth.

"We both live in the same neck of the woods, is all." Seth shrugged, smiling back at Sahara.

"So we better get going if we're going to do some shopping and drop by your shop."

Seth's brown eyes widened. "You want to start now?"

"Yep." Sahara was ready to overpower Seth if he tried to slink out of it. He was going to have this man, and if he had to endure a power reno to do it, he'd man up.

Seth shook his head. "You sure you know what you're getting into?"

"Absolutely," Sahara said, crossing his arms. Shopping first, *then* Seth.

SETH suggested they visit a Moroccan-style warehouse that was set up like an exotic marketplace since Sahara had told him he liked a warm and spicy look. Seth thought that it might be a good place to get an idea, at least, about what Sahara was looking for.

As Sahara drove his friend Jared's beautiful vintage blue DeSoto through the streets, Seth found himself shyly admiring the other man. He was wearing the smoky sunglasses—the same ones he'd had on when he'd taken hold of Seth's sex and ordered him to come—and his blond hair was pulled back in a heavy pewter Celtic clip. Some wisps escaped to touch his tanned forehead.

He was clean shaven, and he smelled really good, like wood and citrus. Seth found himself wanting to lean closer and sniff to try to guess the origin of the scent. The rest of his clothing consisted of a blue shirt over a black tank top and jeans with leather sandals. There was a turquoise beaded hoop around one ankle that was incredibly sexy to Seth for some reason—maybe since he was picturing the bigger man wearing nothing but his handmade jewelry? And he was also wearing the familiar pendant of a square turned upside down so it pointed up at Sahara's chin. It flashed vivid blue as the sun struck through the window.

Seth felt like a quiet little sparrow next to all that lean, mean masculinity, but Sahara acted like he was happy Seth was there, looking at him frequently and once smiling into his eyes before Seth blushed and looked away.

"You have a tattoo of a seashell on your wrist," Seth said, just noticing it now. "Aphrodite?"

Sahara's lips quirked, and he reached out and brushed some of Seth's hair out of his eyes. The movement made Seth's heart give a big *thump.* "You're the only one who has ever recognized the symbolism without me explaining first."

Seth shrugged. "I deal with a lot of marketplaces where language isn't used. Sellers use drawings as allusion to something."

Sahara nodded. "Like in the old days, signs would have had symbols to represent what you could find in shops. I was in Italy not so long ago and spent some time admiring all the phallus symbols carved into the streets of ancient Pompeii."

"Yeah, it's a sexy place to visit if you're a man, imagining what it would have been like, being the slave of some hot Roman master," Seth agreed before he could think about it. Then he realized what he'd said, like something he'd post on Lotus's blog. Shit!

"That *is* sexy. I'd be a very good owner to you, Seth. You'd get lots of use as my slave."

Seth swallowed, trying to push away his secret excitement at the thought. He had to keep his fantasies to himself. "So you said you want to start with your bedroom. Do you want to keep your bed?"

Sahara chewed his lip as they turned in traffic. "I don't know. I am putting myself in your hands, Seth. Do you think it has to go?"

Seth looked out the window rather than at Sahara so he could rein in his thoughts. Bed-plus-Sahara. He had to think of theme, not what had happened between them last night when Sahara had worked himself off on Seth's innocently sleeping body.

"I think it's fine. It has good bones since it is a platform bed, kind of Calvin Klein meets Japan."

"Okay. Suits me since the mattress is pretty new too. I, uh, was always hoping I'd be sharing it with someone for real."

Seth shook his head. "I can't believe a guy who looks like you would want—" He cut himself off, uncertain of his ground. Was he really seeing this man, or was he blinded by his looks? Sahara deserved more. He was upfront, raw.

"Seth, a guy like me wants to come home to someone," Sahara said. His voice deepened. "I really want that. Being alone was okay when I was away a lot of the time, but now it's like one day after the other is a stale TV dinner."

Seth's throat tightened, since he had the same loneliness, but in his case he was so ordinary he didn't think he'd ever attract anyone.

THEY drove past Seth's shop, Sahara slowing down. Seth had a glimpse of pristine windows and his goods in mustard, turquoise, and dark red in the window. Karen must have rearranged the merchandise.

It looked good.

Seth let out a breath he'd been holding and then looked into Sahara's eyes when the other man took his hand and squeezed it in silent empathy.

"OKAY, so this is like 'hot' and 'cold'," Seth said crisply as they entered the cavernous space. "You just tell me what you like, and we can work with that." This was something Seth understood very well, helping a client find colors, textures, things that would enhance their life. Seth enjoyed this, though usually he worked on a far more modest scale. His own home was full of fabrics, leaning toward wool, because despite the warm climate, he often felt chilly. Or maybe, like Sahara, he just felt alone.

Heads turned as they walked past several stands of furniture displays, both men and women looking Sahara over. And this man was interested in Seth? What if... what if Seth believed him and then Sahara got bored with him? Seth knew he'd be shattered. He'd never let anyone close before.

He took a deep breath of the market scent of leather and spices and tried to push aside his fears. They were here to furnish Sahara's floating home, not really as boyfriends.

"I like this," Sahara said, oblivious to Seth's thoughts as he leaned down and touched a Kelim-covered bench in warm tans and greens.

Seth nodded approval. "That would be great up against one of your windows looking out at the harbor. Nice place to sit down sometimes without blocking the view."

Sahara gave a tentative smile and Seth realized that in here, *he* was the man in charge, the one that Sahara looked to. It seemed his new friend hadn't been kidding. He really wanted to make some changes in his life.

"Is there a pattern you like the most?"

Sahara hesitated.

"What one caught your eye first?" Seth coached, knowing that decorating was seriously intimidating to some people. He reached out and clasped Sahara's arm for a moment, stroking it absently.

Sahara looked at his hand and his eyes heated, but then he cleared his throat and glanced back at the ottomans, as if bringing himself back to the task at hand. "I like the one with curling legs."

Seth nodded appreciation. "It's kind of vaguely Elizabethan in design. Nice and warm without being too much, and sturdy as well."

"I'll take it," Sahara said, reaching for his wallet.

"Hey, wait," Seth growled. "Let me do the talking! We might be able to cut you a deal."

Seth was aware of Sahara's bemused smile as he got down to brass tacks with the seller. He felt proud when he got Sahara his discount. This was what he was good at.

"WHAT is this?" Sahara asked him after they passed the spice market where Seth couldn't resist some saffron. He loved to cook rice, sometimes eating only that with some hot butter, and he enjoyed the bright color the spice imparted. Maybe he'd even get a chance to use it one night for his saffron rice pudding to treat Sahara.

"Suzani embroidery, also from Turkey," Seth said, handling the material expertly. "It's a bed cover." It was a deep maroon with blue and white and violet embroidered flowers. It had a masculine feel to it despite the handwork, because of the bold design. He looked at Sahara. "With your love of beading, I can see why you'd like this. It's done on cotton, not silk, so it's probably fairly affordable, and it would go with the Kelim bench you bought."

Seth could see some enthusiasm breaking through Sahara's uncertainty. Seth loved to see his confidence in his choices growing. "Jared is so good at shit like this," Sahara said. "Like you."

"I told you, it's just a muscle you need to exercise," Seth said primly. He was getting a little annoyed at hearing about "Jared this" and "Jared that." Couldn't Sahara see that his own ideas were valid?

"Roger that," Sahara said, some military-speak showing. "If I take that and one of those... flokati rugs, will that work in the bedroom?"

"Ummmm, it'll be really nice. Maybe that watered-down red one that looks like someone took the rug right after it was dyed and put it under a running stream." Seth pointed to a rectangular shag rug, sewn from squares. "It's a little like the sunlight on the water. In fact, all your colors remind me of sunset at your house."

"You like my house," Sahara said, looking proud.

"Your house is amazing!" Seth praised sincerely. "We should think about paint, maybe. You have just white walls with the hardwood. Something like a soft yellow would warm up your bedroom and be good with your new pieces."

"Paint." Sahara blinked.

"Just one room, and I'll help you. There's some clay-based latex paints here that dry very fast without unhealthy fumes."

"So you'll definitely help me paint it?" Sahara prodded. "That might take a while." For some reason, he looked smug.

"I'd like to help you." Seth couldn't refuse those blue eyes.

Again, Sahara smiled.

STANDING in line with his purchases, Sahara put an arm around Seth. Seth stiffened, giving Sahara an uncertain look.

"It's just like decorating, right? Just a muscle you have to work," Sahara reassured him. He leaned down and kissed Seth on the mouth, tender, his tongue caressing Seth's.

Chapter Eight

As SOON as they drove to Seth's shop after dropping by the paint booth where Seth had some saffron-colored paint mixed especially for Sahara's bedroom, Seth caught a bad feeling.

Cute, interested-in-Sahara Officer Martinez was standing outside his shop. Not someone Seth wanted to meet up with again, though he knew that it was inevitable he'd be eclipsed sooner or later in Sahara's eyes. Except worse, as they approached, Seth saw the man wore a grim expression.

Then he saw why.

When he and Sahara had driven by Seth's shop two hours before, the windows had been glistening in the morning sunshine. Seth had figured he'd stop by to check it over before heading back to Sahara's with his loot to help him work on his bedroom.

"Why would someone do this...?" Seth asked. His shop was his baby, a part of him, the realm where he felt confident, as he had when Sahara had asked his decorating advice.

Now, across his formerly pristine windows, the word "Whore" was written in something runny and crimson... something that resembled blood.

"*Fuck!*" Sahara growled as he took in the graffiti. He grabbed Seth close, Seth's back to his front, Sahara's arms firmly around him. Seth could feel the larger man trembling.

Seth swallowed, shaken. *Why was this happening?* "We drove by and it was fine."

Officer Martinez looked sympathetic, despite his sheepish gaze in reaction to the possessive way that Sahara was holding Seth. "Something strange is definitely going on, since the vandalism has happened twice now." He skewered Seth with a look. "Are you sure you have no idea who is doing this? Former boyfriend? Pissed-off employee?"

Seth felt immediately guilty, though he had no idea why. He hadn't a clue why, all of a sudden, someone was breaking his window and leaving the cryptic—and scary—messages.

"No, I don't," he said. "That's not…. It's just paint, right?" The thin quality of the red on the glass made his gut tighten.

Martinez shook his head. "No. The scumbag cut up a stray kitten for the blood, near as I can tell, but it's still alive. I found it crying at the back door of your shop, so I wrapped it in a blanket I carry in my vehicle. The local shelter will probably want to put it down, though…."

"No!" Now Seth felt twice as bad. It had to be the kitten that sometimes came around behind the Dumpster for some milk. Had he attracted the little animal and someone had hurt it as a result? "I have been feeding a stray. It's usually too shy to come near me, or I'd have tried to rescue it."

"Where is it?" Sahara rasped. Seth could feel anger strung tight in the larger man.

"In my squad car." Martinez opened his vehicle door, and Seth's eyes burned. It was the little cat he'd been feeding! He recognized the white mask over the tiny black face. Pale green eyes stared unhappily back up at him.

"This is my fault," Seth whispered, sick.

Sahara's jaw ticked. He had his BlackBerry out and was talking into it a second later. "I found an emergency animal clinic open. Will you trust me to take the kitten there?"

Seth gave Sahara a grateful look. "Sahara…. Yes, please!"

"Don't touch the blood on the window after they're through examining it," Sahara ordered, carefully taking the kitten into his arms, still wrapped in the blanket. The animal mewed piteously but seemed too weak to run away. His white muzzle was bloody. "Fuck, when I find the jerk who did this…!"

Seth wrapped his arms around himself, watching as Sahara placed the kitten in the passenger side of his borrowed car and then got in, the DeSoto moving swiftly into traffic a second later.

"Damn, I'd love to be rescued by him if I wasn't, you know, a macho cop. We could just playact it," Martinez muttered. Then he looked at Seth. "Sorry. Just sayin'."

"He's…." Remarkable. Caring. Protective. Hot as hell. "A nice guy," Seth finished.

"Okay, so you have no idea who is doing this?" Martinez continued. "Because this really seems kind of personal to me. Someone wants to hurt *you*, Seth."

Seth leaned against the cop vehicle. Something niggled at him…. He took a deep breath, frowning as he tried to think.

"Hurting that animal, which you say you were feeding… that tells me that someone must have haunted the area, and he or she might be, uh, practicing in their head to take it further. It sets off some major warning bells, Seth. In fact,"—Martinez's voice lowered—"the person could be watching you now."

Sweat broke out on Seth's forehead and in his armpits at the thought. He looked around, seeing people walking past his shop or loitering on corners. A man reading a magazine whose eyes lifted and caught Seth's….

"It doesn't matter," Seth mumbled. "It's can't be me this person is targeting. It can't." Seth wanted to return to his shop, lock the door, and go upstairs to his rooms. He didn't even want to open on Monday now. He swallowed. "I don't even meet people outside of work."

"Huh. What about Sahara Blue?" Martinez lifted his brows.

SAHARA rubbed tired eyes as the vet, Marsha Thompson, checked over the kitten. "Fortunately the… person who did this didn't cut through anything but the skin on his side," she was saying.

"It's a boy?" Sahara asked.

"Yep. So what do you want me to do? I can stitch him up, but he's suffering from other problems as a result of being a stray."

Sahara's hands were gentle as he caressed the little cat, thinking of Seth's white face. Crap! Who would do this, not only to a defenseless animal, but to innocent Seth?

One thing was for sure: Sahara was not going to fucking let Seth spend any more nights alone in the rooms above his shop. Not until this shit had been settled.

"Give him all he needs. If Seth doesn't want him…." Sahara paused. What the hell was he getting himself into? Yet Jared and Toby were really taken with their Albert, and Sahara's work no longer took him out of the country for unpredictable stretches at a time. "Then I will take him."

Marsha nodded, looking pleased. "All right, then. Got a name for him?"

"I'd like to talk to my… uh, friend first. He may want to do the honors," Sahara said, flushing a little. "I've never had a pet before. Is there a lot of stuff I have to do?"

Marsha smiled. "Okay, I can't wait to meet your friend. And yep, you might find it a bit of an adjustment at first. You may want to get a litter box for him, and you'll need food, vitamins…. He may be anemic. Plus, for now he has to wear a cone over his head to keep from licking those stitches, which he won't like too much."

"I'll get what you recommend, though I think I'll put the litter on the deck outside my front door."

Marsha laughed. "As long as he has access to it. Just remember that he is probably a little feral, so it'll take time for him to build up some trust for you. Cats tend to choose their people."

"Uh-huh," Sahara said, feeling a bit blank. Well, he'd feed the creature.

He fished out his BlackBerry again. He was itching to get back to Seth, not liking the situation one fucking bit. But at least there was one thing he could do.

MAYBE it was a good thing Seth felt so numb when Jared and Toby showed up in Toby's car. He'd been star-struck previously and suffered an embarrassing leg cramp, behaving like a complete dweeb. On any other occasion, he would have been mortified to see them again, done his best to duck away. But now....

Toby cocked his head at Seth and then pulled him into a hug. Seth didn't respond for a moment, experiencing familiar awkwardness. Was he supposed to hug back? Should he be pretending to be okay? He wasn't. The shop… it was his home, his sanctuary, his passion.

"Jared went through a bad time once," Toby whispered, putting an arm around Seth as Jared went over to speak to Officer Martinez. "Someone I knew vandalized his home."

"Oh no!" That cut through Seth's apathy. Hadn't he heard from Sahara over and over again how into his home Jared was?

"Yeah, it was…." Toby's face tightened. "It was a rough time. It took me a long time to forgive myself for bringing that into his life, but… he showed me that to him, having me meant any sacrifice was worth it. We did get a chance to decorate together, just like you and Sahara."

Seth blinked. "I'm helping Sahara out, but I think it's a different thing. We're not…."

"Oh, right!" Toby shook his head. "Sorry. I spent the morning cleaning pools. Sometimes all that chlorine gets to me." His eyes twinkled. "Gives me romantic notions."

"Uh-huh. So why are you and Jared here?" Seth braced himself as Jared returned quietly. The other man moved close to Toby, tall, with longish dark hair and warm brown eyes. He seemed totally centered on his boyfriend, and Seth caught the gleam of matching rings. Man, the two of them appealed to Seth's not-so-carefully buried sentimentality.

"To clean the glass now that Officer Martinez has given his okay," Jared said. "Sahara didn't want you to have to do it."

"Oh." Seth had to clear his throat. "I could have called someone, but… thanks. I really wasn't looking forward to doing it myself."

"Do you have some cleaning stuff?" Jared prodded kindly.

Seth nodded. "I want to take a look around the shop anyway, make sure everything in there is okay."

"Good idea. Toby will go with you," Jared offered. "I'll wait out here. By the way, Sahara wanted you to know the kitten is going to be all right, but he might be another hour making sure he gets proper treatment."

Seth felt his throat tighten. Sahara had definitely been a friend.

"Come on, let's get some Windex and paper towels for Jared, then you can show me what's new in your shop," Toby said.

SETH found everything inside thankfully normal. With the alarms set, it was unlikely anyone could break in, but he was feeling seriously tense, as if an attack could come from any direction.

Toby seemed to enjoy the shop, asking Seth about various stamps and brushes, the cloth he sold that was good for dyeing; silks, cottons, linens, and the waxes used for resist methods.

"I like these marbleized pillows," Toby praised.

"Choose one," Seth said.

Toby's eyes widened.

"No, really, please do," Seth offered. "I want to…." He shrugged, feeling the tension in his shoulders. Shit, if he were alone, he might do something pathetic, like curl up on his bed and just ache. But Sahara and Jared and Toby… they were making it clear he *wasn't* alone.

"Thank you," Toby said. "It'll be nice to have something in our home that was a gift from Sahara's new man."

Seth expelled an exasperated sigh. "I told you that—"

"Right." Toby's face was serene as he chose a Venetian-type traditional marble work, which had a feather pattern achieved by floating paint on water and then using a brush through the dye before laying the cloth on top of the design. It was a simple but beautiful technique that Seth enjoyed teaching.

And now it was going to be featured in Jared and Toby's house. It felt right, even if Toby was mistaken in his ideas about Seth and Sahara.

"TOBY told me I could find you up here." Sahara's voice interrupted Seth's reverie later. Seth was sitting on his bed with his laptop to the side. He'd had an impulse to spill himself out, to express himself, but for the first time, Lotus did not suffice. He felt hemmed in by his identity. His readers came to be tantalized, not to read about broken windows and Seth's fears about what else would happen in future.

"I was trying to…." Seth shrugged. "I can't seem to find a way to forget about stuff. I don't even want to open tomorrow." His shoulders slumped at the admission. Sahara had been a Navy SEAL, an elite warrior. He probably would think Seth wasn't handling himself well.

"What will happen if you don't open?" Sahara sat on the edge of the bed and raised his brows.

"What do you mean?" Seth frowned.

"I mean, if you don't follow routine, who will care? Don't you matter more than this shop?"

"I'm not used to thinking that way," Seth said. "I should—"

"You should take care of yourself, or let *me* do it."

"Sahara...."

"Look, my threat assessment is that whoever this jerk is, he or she is not done. I'd like you to come home and stay with me until we can sort this out."

"How will we?" Seth slammed his laptop shut. "I want my peace of mind back, Sahara! The person who did this shattered more than some glass."

Sahara leaned closer, vivid blue eyes earnest. "I know what it's like to live a 'before' and 'after'. Your life the way you thought it was going to be, the way you liked it, and then...." He shrugged. "But if you give me a little time, I will find this person."

"Officer Martinez said it's almost impossible."

"I was a Navy SEAL," Sahara said. "That word is not in my vocabulary. But in the meantime, I have a kitten without a name and some walls that need painting. And I'm not exactly sure where to put the rug or if I should center the Kelim stool against the windows."

"You're just thinking of stuff to keep me busy."

Sahara raised sandy brows. "If this hadn't happened, I might have tried alcohol, or maybe a late-night movie. Or I might have asked you to cook me dinner and then had no car to see you home."

Seth felt a reluctant smile tug his lips. "What are you saying?"

"I'm saying that...." Sahara cleared his throat. "After last night, I don't want to sleep without you again."

Seth shook his head. "Sahara, you can't be serious!"

"Who says?"

"I mean... about me."

"I'm very serious about you, Seth." Sahara's eyes didn't lie. "This stuff is scaring me, and I want to keep you safe. Will you please let me do that?"

Chapter Nine

SOMETIME later, Seth sat up abruptly on Sahara's bed, running a hand through his hair. His wide eyes focused on Sahara, who was sitting with his knees crossed near the bed. He had a tray with a Japanese thrown teapot and two tea bowls. Nearby, the stray kitten was stretched out on his back, eyes closed.

Sahara was rubbing the cat's nose with his index finger, his expression absorbed.

Pet me.

Seth took a deep breath, willing his body to calm down. He couldn't expect Sahara to treat him the way he did the kitten.

"Nightmare?" Sahara asked calmly, but his eyes burned concern in Seth's direction as he took a sip of his tea. "You were really restless."

Seth was sure his blush would give him away. He felt like his whole body was pulsing neon pink. "No, not exactly."

Sahara quirked an eyebrow. "Another kind of dream?" he purred.

Seth looked down at his hands, kneading the sheet that covered Sahara's bed. They hadn't put out the new bedspread or other things yet, since they wanted to paint first, but when they'd first arrived at Sahara's place, Seth had felt completely wiped, like he needed to curl in the fetal position and just sleep. Somehow Sahara had seemed to sense it, because he'd guided Seth into his room, told him to strip, and folded down the bedding before disappearing with the new kitten, muttering about litter boxes.

Now Seth was awake, and even though he was embarrassed by his dream, he was glad for the company and the distraction from his problems. Maybe Sahara wasn't the only one who didn't want to sleep alone again, although sleeping with Sahara.... Until he'd actually done it, it had seemed as likely as winning the lottery. He was having trouble believing this could be real.

"Seth, what did you dream about?" Sahara's voice was intimate, caressing. Boyfriend to boyfriend.

Seth's chest tightened as he responded instinctively. "I dreamt that you found a rather, uh, unique way to show me that I'm attractive to you."

A second later, Seth wondered what he was doing, confessing that to Sahara. He was not Lotus. He could not share this part of himself. He wasn't removed enough, locked away in an anonymous cyber world. Instead he was right here, face to face, where rejection would be devastating.

Sahara shifted so he was beside Seth, kneeling by the bed. He was so tall that he was eye-level with him. "Seth...."

Seth blew out another breath. "Okay, it was a sexy dream."

"I was featured in one of your sexy dreams?" Sahara looked pleased, and his expression was accessible, so that Seth was startled into realizing that this man might also be vulnerable.

"Yes, you've been starring in them since I met you," Seth admitted, swallowing thickly. Since before then, but how could he tell Sahara that? Tell him he'd looked for him, found him; that he was Lotus.

"I like to be on top." Sahara's voice was suggestive.

Seth quirked an eyebrow, suddenly amused, like feeling sunlight coming into a dark corner. This was what Sahara did for him. "You definitely are in my fantasies."

Sahara's vivid blue eyes were heavy-lidded as he held Seth's. "Tell me," he prodded. "Tell me how I had you, baby."

"You didn't... quite." Seth's cheeks burned, but he couldn't seem to stop himself from sharing. The secret part of himself wanted Sahara to truly know him, to touch him. "You were in control, though." His eyelashes fell. "Almost in ownership."

Sahara's chest was rising and falling more rapidly, and Seth could see the pulse thumping in his neck. His lips parted. "Seth, don't tease me. I am so turned on."

Seth closed his eyes, seeing it play out again in his mind. Hot! "I had one of those kind of asleep, kind of awake fantasies," he admitted.

"Mmmmm," Sahara encouraged him to go on.

"I dreamt that you took me to some kind of fancy mansion. It was hosting a special party." Seth's eyes opened. "In my fantasy, I'm innocent and we haven't—"

Sahara reached out with a gentle hand, combed Seth's hair away from his face. "Like we are now. I haven't been inside you yet."

Seth gave a tight nod. "I'm not sure I believe you when you tell me that you find me attractive, so you decide to do something about it. You escort me into this house and then give me a plastic bag and instruct me to change into what is inside in a bathroom." Seth saw that Sahara's pupils were huge, as if he were a focused predator. "I do as you ask, though when I find out what's in the bag...!"

"What is it?" Sahara demanded, obviously enthralled.

"It's light blue briefs made of silk," Seth revealed. "Not feminine, exactly, but made for a man who wants to feel...."

"Like the bottom for his top," Sahara added, obviously wanting to be part of the story, to weave himself into the experience with Seth.

"Yes," Seth said, though color still stung his cheeks. It helped to see that Sahara was also flushed. The tips of his ears were a bright pink, which was kind of adorable on such a macho man.

"You put them on for me?" Sahara asked in a deep voice.

"Yes," Seth breathed. "There is also a matching silk robe in the bag. I put that on as well, feeling the cool material against my skin. It makes my nipples hard and my…."

"*You're* hard, putting on the underwear, the robe," Sahara filled out.

"When I come into the hallway, you're…." Seth gave a little shrug. "Like you are now. Intense."

"I'll bet," Sahara said. "So what do I do with you next?"

"You lead me into what is kind of like one of those smoking parlors, where gentlemen drink port and smoke cheroots or cigars."

"Like a gentleman's club. Very sexy."

"This one has a twist; black round tables beside each leather club chair." Was he really going to share this? But he was as caught up as Sahara now, the intimacy of storyteller and listener. It was something that Seth lived as Lotus, but he'd never thought he'd ever get to express this part of himself in real life.

"Let me guess, it's a pedestal for my very special pet."

Seth nodded shyly.

"I tell you to let the robe fall, and when it does… the round, pale shape of your shoulders. I'm spellbound. Just that slow hint of your body. Man!"

"I let it fall like a geisha trained to please," Seth said, enjoying this fantasy far more now that Sahara had walked inside it, was playing with him. In cyberspace, this kind of dance was limited, though until now he hadn't known.

"You are the perfect pet. I've brought you tonight to show you off, how proud I am of you, how hot you make me."

Seth smiled, pleased, even though it was nothing they'd ever really done together. "After the robe falls, I hop onto the table and lean forward."

Sahara stepped up to the plate, taking his part, taking control: "I run my hand down your back. Oh, and I'm wearing black leather gloves."

Seth shivered, as if he could feel that ghost touch.

Sahara laughed, clearly having fun, before continuing in a husky tone. "I lower your silky underwear, exposing most of the moons of your ass, and as I do a few other connoisseurs approach and watch."

Seth was breathing hard. Shit! He had broken out in a sweat. Sahara's lips were close. He ached for a kiss. "Do they want to touch me?" he asked.

Sahara reached out, cupped Seth's cheek, and his eyes were full of a poignant kind of tenderness now. "Yes, Seth. How could they resist you? You're so sexy with your pale back and great ass. Everyone wants to be me."

"You do have me, you know," Seth said, pushing his face against Sahara's broad, warm hand. His protector. His friend. He felt as safe with him as the tiny cat, snoring on his back on the floor while Seth and Sahara played.

Sahara took a deep breath. "I tie your wrists with a silk scarf, and then I sit down to savor some of that brandy. And when one of the other men comes over to see you, it's up to me whether or not he is permitted to touch you, to stroke you, or even to put his fingers inside you where you are lubed and receptive."

"Sahara…," Seth moaned.

"You sound just like that as some tall, dark, and handsome stranger finger-fucks you while I watch."

Seth squirmed on the bed. The game had gone too far. He needed—

Sahara tossed aside the sheet, suddenly also impatient, exposing Seth's modest T-shirt and underwear-clad body. He reached and Seth moved forward at the same time, and then Seth's plain white briefs were pushed aside and Sahara's hand enclosed him firmly, warmly. A man's hand, handling him, knowing exactly how to work him.

"Oh God, Sahara!" Seth was panting, hands balled at his sides, lower body thrust wantonly forward, begging for Sahara's attentions.

"That's it, boy. I control this." Sahara's thumb smoothed over Seth's cockhead, and fresh moisture pearled at the tip. "I control you, don't I?"

"Yes, Sahara," Seth whispered, eyes caught by Sahara's gaze as his hand moved up and down, slow, teasing. In a softer voice, he added something else.

Sahara's vivid blue eyes narrowed, his matching pendant banging against his chest as he growled, "Say it louder. Repeat it."

"Yes... master," Seth breathed, gaze falling. He couldn't believe he'd said *those* words, but he'd been waiting all his life for the man who would make him want to.

"Oh shit, that's hot." Sahara's lips grazed his as he continued to tug at Seth's penis, bringing another helpless moan from Seth's lips.

"Please, please...," Seth pleaded.

"It's mine. I decide." Sahara licked Seth's lips, a slow outline of the hot, parted shape.

"Yes. God, yes, I want that...."

"You need to be someone's boy." Sahara pulled away but then pushed Seth on his back, tugging his legs so his ass was on the edge of the bed, his legs spread and open while Sahara knelt in the V. The larger man reached down, took Seth's cock again.

Seth sagged back, toes curling, head twisting on the pillow. Sahara, his master, would decide when he came.

SAHARA felt like he'd entered one of Lotus's fantasies. The story had been so fucking hot, and then Seth had surrendered in the way he had when he'd knelt behind Sahara and put his lips to the deep scarring on Sahara's back.

God, he'd sealed his fate then, if he'd only known it. Sahara had wanted to drag him by the hair to some warm cave, open his legs, and hammer into him.

Now he was aching to be inside Seth. What would it feel like to ride him while holding his eyes? Sahara had never had a boyfriend, but he'd seen plenty of the closeness exchanged between Jared and Toby, and he wanted that for himself. Seth was perfect for him, as if he were a mate genetically engineered in some lab who exactly matched Sahara's needs.

When Seth's legs suddenly wrapped around Sahara's hips, he let out a long groan. "You're asking for it, slut," he whispered.

Seth grinned a little, face glowing, sweaty, while his penis was firmly in Sahara's hand. He obviously liked being under Sahara's control, liked being his slut.

"I think I left out one thing I might do to my boy on the table," Sahara gritted. He was going to spill his come on Seth. One way or another.

"What?" Seth asked, wide-eyed, anticipating, tongue teasing his lips, teasing Sahara.

"I think I'd take my glove off and have you lift that saucy ass so I could spank it for you. What do you think of that?"

Seth gave a thready sound, looking far gone, his pupils blown, his body shivering violently at every stroke. He was riding the edge.

"Come, boy," Sahara encouraged.

Seth's head fell back and he stiffened, spending himself in Sahara's grip, his body lovely, truly perfect as he gave himself.

"Sahara," he called out, making it totally clear who was his fantasy, who he obeyed. "Oh, Sahara...."

Sahara couldn't wait! It felt like a band wrapped around his head, his chest, and his prick was so hard he thought he'd burst in his pants. Sahara shed them quickly and then stood up by the bed, a little shaky after what he'd guided Seth through, but needing—

His come hit Seth's lips, his chin and neck as he lay back, used, content, rosy. When Seth licked the taste of his spend, Sahara got on the bed, climbed on Seth so his spent penis nudged his lips. "Lick it all," he ordered.

Chapter Ten

"Sahara?"

"Ummm." Warm skin, nice hair. His arms wrapped around someone lean with the perfect place to rest his chin. Heaven.

"The kitten… I think he's hungry."

Sahara blinked. Kitten? He didn't have a—

Oh. Shit.

He sat up, seeing mussed Seth, his briefs pulled up, but they were both—

"We need a shower."

Seth turned pink.

Sahara wanted to groan. Why was it he could give the other man a hand job and then he retreated again? But then his jaw hardened. Okay, so Seth was a bit of work, but he was more than worth it. "Take the shower, I'll strip the bed and go in after you. Then maybe we can sort out what to feed him. Uh, and we need a name."

Seth rolled over, his brown eyes like melting chocolate in the mellow light of late afternoon off the water. This was just the way Sahara wanted Seth looking at him. It made him appreciate having the other man here, receptive and touchable and his. "I think you should name him."

"You do?"

"Yeah."

Sahara stared up at the pattern of water making wavy, moving lines on the ceiling above where he rested with Seth. "Maybe… Lotus."

Seth stiffened in his arms. "Why that name?"

Sahara shrugged, not wanting to explain. What if Seth thought he was a weirdo for being attracted to someone online? What if it made the other man even more insecure? Sahara decided to keep his thing with Lotus a secret. And tempting as the fantasy was, maybe he'd stop visiting the site, because warm skin, soft hair…. There was nothing like the real thing.

"We better get up, do stuff, feed Lotus."

HIS hair wet against his neck from his recent shower, Seth held the little animal while Sahara carefully put an antibiotic ointment on the line of stitches on the kitten's side. When the cat wasn't sleeping or under their watchful eye, he had to wear a cone around his head to keep from worrying at the stitches. Unfortunately, it made him cry piteously.

The sound seemed to get under Seth's breastbone. Sahara looked up and Seth could see the same bafflement and pain in his eyes. Neither of them could understand hurting a little creature this way.

Seth was moved to reach for Sahara's hand, though he blushed and let his fingers drop before he made contact. What they'd shared…. He couldn't believe he'd been that intimate with Sahara. Not just what they'd done, but what they'd talked about, the fantasy they'd shared.

"You did an amazing thing for this little guy, taking care of him."

"You would have done the same," Sahara said serenely.

Seth held Sahara's eyes. "Yes, I would have. Especially since this is my fault in the first place."

Sahara's eyes heated to turbulent blue, like the windswept tide coming in the harbor. "No, Seth. Some sicko did this to a kitten and to you, and I will, by God, find him and give him a *very* bad day."

"I can't believe I'm here with you," Seth reflected. "And suddenly you have a kitten. And I'm helping you decorate and… stuff."

Sahara shook his head, a look of tender amusement moving through the blue eyes. "And stuff. Oh, yeah." He pointed out the window toward the floating home opposite. Soft mandolin music moved lazily across the water, and Seth could see lanterns lit along the side of the house. He blinked, remembering what he'd had on the agenda just days ago, before the vandalism, before he'd met Sahara Blue. He'd been planning to decorate his shop soon, since the holidays were rapidly approaching.

"That's what I want. I've wanted it for a long time."

"Yeah?" But his first thought was, *Enough to settle?* Seth chewed his lip.

"I am going to take you to affirmation classes if you keep that up," Sahara said, as if he could read that thought. "I like you. I want you here."

Seth felt warmth move through him, as free and easy as one of his dye cloths drying outside on the line he'd strung between brick buildings, swaying in the sunshine and wind. "I like you too," he said.

THEY sorted out the kitten's food by seeing what he'd eat. He was a little fussy, whether from stress or because he was a stray. The vet had advised them to start small and to make sure he had accessible food that was always kept fresh.

Then Sahara heated up his tea kettle, since his coffeemaker was still not working, and they drank Earl Grey from mugs as they looked over the bare walls in Sahara's bedroom. The bed and statue and the one low dresser Sahara had moved safely out of the way into the center of the room.

"You up to this?" Sahara prodded. "We don't have to do this today."

Seth expelled a breath. "I don't want to think. I don't want to be afraid." His muscles tightened sometimes, seemingly all on their own, and he had to consciously tell himself not to think about what had happened at his shop, the bedrock of his life. He'd been there for years and never had any trouble. But now trouble had found him, and he felt exposed and vulnerable. Naked.

He was also naked with Sahara, which made him want to retreat under a rock and nurse his feelings. Somehow Sahara seemed to get that, since he busied them with caring for the kitten and sipping tea and putting down plastic drop cloths and taping off the floor and removing switch plates.

"You use the roller and I'll cut in the trim," Sahara suggested. He handed Seth the flat tray with paint and then stood watching as he tentatively began the first coat.

"Nice… not paint smell," Sahara noted. "Smells like the earth beside a stream bed."

Seth smiled at the wet-clay fragrance clouding the air. In less than fifteen minutes with this type of paint, it would be dry and there would barely be any fumes. And then he could do the second coat.

"I used this color in the shop. Everything looks great against it."

The work made him break out in a sweat, but it was good, finding his rhythm, watching the saffron go on cold white walls, warming the space. He loved working with paint, whether dyes or something on a wall. It was always satisfying, changing something for the better.

"I think we'll only need two coats," he noted. "Since the base was white to begin with." He looked at Sahara, who was cutting in around the windows. The bigger man had removed his T-shirt and wore it around his hair as a rough headband. His bare chest was rippling with muscle, and his pendant beat a tattoo steadily between his pointed nipples. Oh, boy. Seth swallowed and continued with what composure he could manage, "Are you going to paint the other rooms?"

Sahara nodded. "Not right away, but yeah. I'd like to do it all and then maybe… I don't know, I have driftwood and seashells up top on my patio, and some shit I've collected while diving various places, like an old glass bottle covered in barnacles. I'd like to make something up there, maybe grow some herbs that would be nice for cooking. Jared does that."

Seth raised an eyebrow. "So you're going to go for it, take up cooking."

"Um. Why not? I might not end up being much of a cook, but I'd like to cook for you."

"All right," Seth said, feeling suddenly serene. "I'd like to see you try."

They smiled at each other, and the moment glowed between them, heated, like when they touched.

THEY moved in tandem, like a team of college painters who had been doing this for a while, earning money for tuition. Seth rested once the first coat was on with the roller, watching Sahara deal with the far fussier job of avoiding the trim, which looked to be a white oil-based paint. It was fine to go with the color they were laying down, a warm yellow that lit the space like stray sunbeams. It immediately felt right to Seth, and he noticed Sahara making satisfied sounds every now and then, as if he liked what they were accomplishing.

"So I was thinking maybe we'd go visit my friend Jai up north," Sahara said, super casual.

Seth stiffened. "I have the store to open tomorrow…."

"Look, Seth, I need time to set some stuff up to catch this asshole," Sahara said. "I'd like to set up a surveillance camera in a discreet location, and I've been thinking of eyeballing the place myself, maybe get a couple of friends to trade off shifts with me." He continued flatly, "It will be all over once I see him."

"But how will you recognize him?" Seth asked, uncertain.

"I have pretty well-honed instincts," Sahara said, again displaying that assured confidence. "I'll know him. And I'll take him down."

"We're sure he's a guy?"

"Yeah, just has that vibe. Almost acts like a betrayed lover or something, but you haven't—"

Seth shook his head vehemently. "No, there's no one."

"Suits me," Sahara said, looking a little smug at the confirmation. "But if you stay in Mendocino with my friend Jai, I don't need to worry about protecting you while I take this guy down."

Mendocino. Jai. Take down. Surveillance.

"I live in a safe rut," Seth said, licking dry lips, the fear living under his ribs now, nudging him every now and then and taking him from his safety zones. He didn't want to go stay with a stranger. It took all his courage to just be with Sahara. "I am adventurous in the colors I choose, in the rugs I import in shades and patterns that move me." And in his online persona, but he couldn't confess that to Sahara now. "And I'm working on being that way with this… thing with you, Sahara."

Sahara put down the brush and went to Seth, studying him soberly before pulling him into his arms. Immediately Seth felt encompassed by Sahara's concern. "All right?" Sahara rumbled.

"Better than all right," Seth sighed. "I've opened the shop every Monday to Saturday for…."

"It's just this little while. Life isn't always a straight line, you know?" Sahara coached gently.

"I think when I met you, possibly you busted my compass," Seth said ruefully.

"You busted mine too. So we'll talk about you visiting my friend maybe after dinner." Obviously Sahara was not going to let it go.

Seth sighed, "I'd really rather stay here. You saw how pathetic I was meeting Jared and Toby. I'm not good with new people unless it's in my shop."

"Well, you could maybe stay over with Jared and Toby when I was at work if you'd prefer. I just have this feeling the nut job is focused on *you*, and it makes me uneasy." Sahara picked up the brush again. "I like this saffron color. You gonna make me that rice pudding you talked about?"

Seth nodded. "As soon as I lay down the second coat."

"Okay, then." Sahara looked pleased.

ONCE the second coat was almost dry, just a little cool to the touch of a bare hand, Seth started seriously working on their treat. He added cinnamon, raisins, and brown sugar to the simmering yellowed rice in the pot, catching the clump of heavy footsteps on the ladder outside that led to the rooftop patio just before Sahara appeared, flushed from the fresh air, eyes as brilliant as his signature beaded pendant.

Sahara kissed Seth's cheek, and Seth flushed himself, but with delight, not fresh air. Was this what it was like to have a real boyfriend?

"Salmon needs another few minutes. I like it so tender that it falls apart in the butter."

Seth's mouth watered at the thought. "I made a salad," he said, nodding to one made of the sort of sad romaine lettuce he'd found in Sahara's fridge. The tomatoes he'd had to cut the mold off first and rescue the best parts, but it wasn't too bad.

"Looks fantastic!" Sahara reached for a piece, white teeth crunching the greens with satisfaction. He was a really primal guy, and watching him do something as simple as eat made Seth's stomach twist. *Want.* He wanted Sahara.

"There's some beer in the fridge," Sahara continued, digging it out. "Man, this is turning out to be just about the perfect day." He looked at Seth. "And night."

"It was nice," Seth said. He was still feeling timid, but he wanted Sahara to know his attentions were welcome. Appreciated.

"Waking up with you in my arms." Sahara's voice deepened. "Not to mention coming on you."

Seth's head ducked, and he stirred the rice pudding a little faster.

Sahara gave a soft laugh. "Can we move stuff into my bedroom after dinner?"

Seth was grateful for the change of topic. "I think so. Paint is about cured now."

"Good. I want to get all the new shit into place. I want you to like my bedroom," Sahara said.

Chapter Eleven

"STAY here in the kitchen," Sahara directed after taking down the green painter's tape and gathering up the drop cloths and other mess. He had a conspiratorial look in his eyes, reminding an amused Seth of someone hiding a holiday gift. "I mopped the floor. Hardwood looks good with the color."

"You want me to see your bedroom after it's set up?" Seth couldn't help but shake his head. He seemed to be getting more comfortable with this man in a hurry—and just a day ago he'd been sure he'd never see him again. The search for things for Sahara's home and the painting had worked wonders, which made him wonder if that had somehow been Sahara's intention all along. "It's fine, go ahead; I need to watch the pudding so the rice doesn't stick and burn."

Just then, Seth's BlackBerry buzzed.

"And get your phone," Sahara called, heading back into his room. As Seth answered, he heard the rustle of furniture being moved. Would they sleep together again in Sahara's newly redone bedroom?

"Hello?" he answered.

A voice rasped, "*I know you're with him, Lotus. Don't you think you should go home?*"

"Who is this?" Seth demanded. The voice was male, Seth was sure of it, despite the way the caller was whispering.

The line went dead.

Heart pounding, Seth put his BlackBerry back in his pocket.

Lotus. The man had called him Lotus.

"Who was it?" Sahara called.

"No one," Seth answered. He took a deep breath and stirred the saffron rice pudding.

"YOU *have* to tell him, Seth." Karen's voice was very firm over the phone as Seth paced on the garden top roof of Sahara's floating home. He'd needed to confide in someone after the call shook him up, so he'd rung Karen for advice. "I don't understand why you haven't."

"He actually seems to like me. Seth. Plain, *boring* me."

"You are not—"

"I'm just a shopkeeper. Lotus is... alluring, sexually confident; everything I'm not." Seth shoved his hair back, throat tightening. "No one ever noticed *me*. I'd go to bars and someone would always take the blond home, or the muscled guy, or the guy with more tattoos.... If I managed to get a word in, I'd get stared through. Sahara looked at me. He really seems to like me, believe it or not."

"Seth." Karen's voice gentled. "You were really young when you first hit the scene, unsure of yourself, of coming out. I know you're very sensitive and you were hurt, but you can't live through Lotus. I've been praying for you to meet a nice guy, someone who would give you something better to do with your time than type up your fantasies to share with a bunch of anonymous strangers. They won't ever be there at night when you're alone. And they won't be there when you have the flu, you know?"

"But if I tell him...." Seth rubbed his forehead. "It'll ruin everything. First, he'll know I was lying by omission." Seth swallowed. "And then... what if he dumps me as Seth? At least I'd still hold him as Lotus."

"What?" Karen blurted. "Seth, that's twisted! You have to be honest with him if you want a *real* thing. And you shouldn't assume he's going to dump you."

"Why would he want me?" Seth asked. "I still don't understand."

"Okay, *enough*," Sahara's voice interrupted. He was standing with his muscled arms folded at the edge of the balcony. He looked seriously intimidating.

Seth paled. How much had the other man heard him tell Karen? "Karen, I have to go," he said quickly, cutting the connection. "You were listening?"

"I was thinking of stirring the coals in the hibachi, and I caught you saying that you didn't know why I'd want you."

Seth looked at his feet. He had no idea what to say. His vulnerability and lack of confidence was the elephant suddenly standing between them. "Yeah."

"You don't get it."

Seth's jaw tightened. It felt like Sahara was rubbing it in, but his blue eyes were steady, demanding Seth meet them. "No," he said.

"I guess I'm going to have to teach you," Sahara said. "You know when you become a SEAL, you build on confidence like muscle. After a while, you feel like you can take on the world."

"I'm nothing like you." Seth turned away, looking out at the harbor. "I don't even know why I'm here. Sure, someone seems to be hassling me but... this isn't real. This isn't my life."

"It is if you want me," Sahara whispered.

Seth turned around at that to look at him, but he only caught a glimpse of Sahara's tanned hands on the loops of the ladder as the other man headed back to the first level of his floating home, leaving Seth on his own.

HANDS dug into his pockets and shoulders hunched, Seth hesitated outside Sahara's bedroom door. Sahara was stripped down to a white tank top, slightly damp, and Malibu shorts. He was bent over something on the floor by the windows looking out at the harbor, which at first Seth took for maybe a musical instrument.

Sahara looked up, as if he sensed Seth standing there, but then his attention returned to his project.

Hesitant, Seth walked into the room. He knew how he felt when he was hurting. He'd just never imagined he'd have the power to hurt someone else.

"Oh, a dreamcatcher," Seth said as he came closer to where Sahara was seated. "I was hoping you'd teach me how to make one."

"If I do, that means I don't have to teach any classes, right?" Sahara's tone was absent. He had a long branch in one hand, and as Seth watched he bent it to form a circle.

"Surely in the SEALs you had to teach sometimes?" Seth asked. The dreamcatcher in progress felt like it might be an olive branch. Seth wanted to take it.

Sahara looked up with wide blue eyes. "I was a firearms instructor. A medic. This is… crafts."

Seth grinned. "Afraid of a few old ladies?"

Sahara shook his head. "Out of my depth."

Seth said, "I know what that feels like."

Sahara held his gaze before his own dropped back to the budding creation. "Now I've secured the circle, I wrap this suede twine around it," he outlined, as if teaching Seth how to make a dreamcatcher was easier, and safer, than talking to him.

Seth swallowed, dropping his head. He'd done that. His lack of confidence in himself had somehow darkened the waters between him and Sahara.

"So you started making these for your dexterity?" he asked, wanting to draw the other man out again.

Sahara shrugged, avoiding Seth's eyes. "I, uh, can be sleep-challenged sometimes."

"Oh."

"You've seen my back."

Seth remembered the gluey texture of Sahara's skin, the deep grooves. He had a strange impulse to lift his shirt and trace the lines now, as if he had the right. "So you work on this when you can't sleep?"

Sahara huffed out a laugh. "I work on it so my hands will stop shaking." He looked at Seth and then looked away.

"Sahara," Seth whispered, unable to keep his distance. Drawn closer, he put his hand on Sahara's shoulder, feeling warm skin, muscle, and the tail end of one scar that snaked up from his back.

"You sealed your fate when you kissed my back," Sahara warned, eyes narrowed.

"I'll take the risk." Seth looked at Sahara's lips, and then his eyes, and then those lips covered his, and Sahara made a soft sound as he yanked Seth closer, the unborn dreamcatcher falling aside.

"How can you think I don't really want you? Do you think I sleep with any guy?"

Seth blinked, lips freshly crushed, hand sliding down Sahara's arm. "No, I figure you don't want anyone to know about your, um, insomnia." He figured it was a better way of putting it than nightmares.

Sahara nodded. "Right. You're the only exception. If you hadn't made the mistake of touching my back, I would have stuck to the couch." His lips twisted. "Well, for a while, anyway."

Seth stroked flesh through Sahara's tank, and Sahara gusted out a sigh. "Yeah. Like that, baby. You are so fucking hot."

Unable to hold Sahara's serious blue eyes, Seth looked around, color high in his cheeks. "You put everything in place," he said, noting the Balinese lady sitting by the low bed and the new pieces they'd chosen together. It felt like a space they'd created to share as lovers.

Had that been why Sahara had invited him to help out? No, it couldn't be. He was just ordinar—

Catching the spiraling direction of his own self-doubt, Seth said, "I need to build my confidence."

"I'll help you with that, if you want." Sahara's lips dragged against Seth's, delicate friction that made Seth's backbone feel heavy.

"Yeah, uh…." Seth drifted. "Oh, shit! My rice pudding…!" Seth got to his feet with regret. He'd completely forgotten their dessert. But looking into Sahara's vivid blue eyes, he thought maybe he should just let the rice burn because *here* was yummy.

His BlackBerry buzzed, so he dug it out of his pocket and glanced at the text message.

I warned you to go back home where you belong.

"Shit!" He felt ice feather his spine where warmth had kissed it. "Sahara, the guy hassling me—" He took a deep breath, handing his BlackBerry over to Sahara. "Listen, I have to tell you something."

Sahara read the message and his face hardened. He got to his feet, reaching into a drawer and pulling out a harness and gun. Narrowed blue eyes glared in Seth's direction. "Stay here, baby," he was ordered.

"Sahara!"

Sahara strode from the room.

Heart pounding, Seth felt like pulling his hair. No, he felt like pulling *Sahara's* hair.

What? He was supposed to stay here while the man he was very… fond of put himself in danger? Granted, he was a shopkeeper, not a big, bad ex-Navy SEAL who made his living protecting VIPs, but—

He had drifted back to the kitchen in Sahara's wake, and now he found himself staring into the contents of the pot he'd had simmering. Yep, glue. He turned off the heat, took the pudding, and poured water on it in Sahara's sink.

"Like fuck I'll stay here," he muttered.

Chapter Twelve

OKAY, so maybe Seth didn't have much confidence in himself as a man—although he intended to change that. If Sahara wanted him, he would not fuck it up. And maybe he knew nothing about stalkers and surveillance and the world that Officer Martinez and Sahara lived in. But he'd worked very hard on his store, pouring so much of himself into it. He was not going to let anyone take that away from him.

When he reached the parking lot, it was to discover that Sahara had borrowed Jared's car again, racing off to investigate. Fine, so he wasn't going anywhere fast, but he'd get there just the same.

Seth stalked up the steep hill toward his shop, passing a few owners closing their familiar businesses for the day. Some recognized him and nodded, making Seth feel safer. It wasn't like he was unknown in this neighborhood. He nodded back absently while his mind raced.

His stalker knew he was Lotus.

The realization gaped like a big hole. Seth could barely take it in when he thought of all the intimate things he'd written about, never mind that lately he'd been inspired by one man, Sahara Blue. But he'd always had an audience, and one of them had obviously taken it far more seriously than he'd ever imagined.

GECKO SHELDON was waiting for him when Sahara swung Jared's car into a parking slot near Seth's shop. He got out of the DeSoto and nodded to the shorter man, his swim buddy from when he'd been a SEAL. Gecko quirked a brow at him, wearing sunglasses and typically messy beachwear. His red hair was sticking straight up, and he was unshaven.

"Long time, man," Gecko noted. "You woke me up when you called. I was napping in my dinghy, just rockin'."

"Yeah, I can see that," Sahara said. "A friend of mine has a problem."

"I got here about three minutes ago. Thought I saw a light on upstairs. Your friend's not home?"

Sahara tensed, giving Seth's darkened shop a cautious look. When he'd been picking up the things for his home under Seth's enthusiastic tutelage, he'd seen how much his shop had to mean to him. It was his passion. "Shit."

"So we're going in?" Gecko's brown eyes were lit with anticipation as he took off his shades, all business. "If you're not packing, I brought a little something I can lend you."

A little something from Gecko could be anything, including a rocket launcher. He was definitely the guy you wanted to bring to this kind of party. "No, I'm good," Sahara said, feeling sweat slicking the back of his neck, but his hands were steady, and something clicked into place, like his body was a machine going on autopilot.

"Cool," Gecko said.

"RUDY!" Seth huffed, having almost run into the older man two shops down from his own. Fruit exploded from a box Rudy had been carrying back inside, miniature oranges, tangerines, bouncing like balls on the steep slope. "Oh shit, I'm sorry!"

Seth reached down, grabbed three oranges, and tossed them back in their package. From where he was helping Rudy, he could see Jared's vintage car parked at the curb just ahead. There was no sign of

Sahara Blue. Was he inside the shop? But he couldn't be, since Seth had never given him a key or the alarm code... could he?

Seth chewed his lip, unsure what exactly an ex-Navy SEAL was capable of.

"S-Seth," Rudy stuttered. "Seth, help me?"

"Rudy, by any chance have you seen anyone around my shop tonight?" Seth asked, wanting to push on and find Sahara but unable to leave Rudy with all the fruit to deal with. He knelt and picked up more tangerines.

"N-no one but me. And you." Rudy only shook his head, greasy dark hair falling in his hazel eyes as he picked up more oranges from the street. "H-have to wash these."

"I'm sorry I didn't see you, Rudy." Seth got to his feet. Was Sahara around back of his shop?

"Me too," Rudy said. "But you never see me, do you, S-Seth?"

Seth felt immediately guilty. He tried to be nice. He knew what it was like to be awkward around people. "Hey, Rudy...."

Rudy shrugged. "It's okay." He held out a fruit shyly. "Here, have one, Seth."

Seth took the tangerine automatically, though he didn't want it. He gasped, yanking his hand back, dropping the gift. His palm was bleeding. "Rudy...."

Rudy tugged Seth close to him, as if he and Seth were two dancers running through the tango. Rudy's eyes were intent on Seth's face.

"What...?" Seth felt hot, woozy. Without Rudy holding onto him, he would fall like the fruit from his hand. Splat.

"I'll help you, Seth," Rudy whispered. He shocked Seth by pressing a small kiss against his lips.

"No, uh—" The street was revolving like he was on one of those rides that always made him sick after the first five minutes. He used to love them, but once he was in his twenties....

He noticed Rudy's employer was still working—Mr. Chalmers, the elderly man who owned the vegetable and fruit stand. He could see him just inside the glass, cashing out. A pedestrian walked by, bumping Seth so he nearly fell over.

"H-help," Seth croaked, his lips feeling rubbery.

Rudy kicked the box of retrieved oranges closer to the other fruits, smiling gently as he led Seth into the alley by his shop.

The brick was unforgiving as Seth smacked into it, wobbly. His heart was pounding like a drum in his ears. He licked his lips. "Rudy... please."

"It's time for you to come with me, Lotus." Rudy's stutter was gone. He looked suddenly awake to Seth, as if he'd been sleeping all this time. He stood straighter and his eyes were sharp, penetrating. Seth couldn't take it in. Rudy? Rudy left treats out for the kitten. Rudy always blushed when Seth talked to him.

Rudy was his stalker?

Rudy stared at Seth from across the width of the alley, watching as Seth struggled to keep to his feet, fingers scrabbling over dirty brick.

As Seth wavered, Rudy unhurriedly removed his mustache and goatee, peeling them off.

"Noooo," Seth said. "No. Sahara."

"Ah ah," Rudy said, taking hold of Seth by his hair, twisting the strands so Seth cried out.

Rudy covered Seth's open mouth with his own, his tongue invading, taking possession. The kiss went on for a long time, Seth sagging against the wall, too weak to resist.

Seth could feel Rudy was hard through his jeans. "Uhhuhhh!" Tears welled in Seth's eyes. He bit Rudy's tongue.

A fist crashed into his lower belly, and Seth choked, struggling to breathe. Pain bloomed a second later in his cheek. He couldn't lift his hand to touch the hurt, just blinked up at Rudy. A Rudy without his stutter. A Rudy without his goatee.

"Bit you back," Rudy said, hand around Seth's throat like a choke collar so Seth coughed. Oh, God. Rudy could strangle him and Seth couldn't fight him off!

Seth was coated in cold, dripping sweat. It was hard work just breathing, his heart pounding so hard.

Rudy swung him around, and Seth gagged, dizzy, his head feeling like it was still revolving, like it was a fallen orange, running down the hill, picking up speed.

"THE alarm was a piece of cake to bypass," Gecko noted with an undertone with disdain. "Almost as easy as picking the lock on the back door. You ought to tell your pal."

"Boyfriend," Sahara corrected equally softly. "And I'm planning on it." He'd never hidden who he was from Gecko. Gecko had never made any comment about Sahara's orientation, but he also never talked about his own personal life, so that tracked.

Now, as Sahara let the back door kiss gently closed behind them both, the tiny sound seemed to echo extra loud. He flashed back to his first meeting with Seth, so recent. He'd barely taken in the shop because it had been like that effect used in movies, zooming in on a dolly to focus on Seth so that sounds, sights, all were muffled. There was only Seth.

Yet even without Seth here, the place was warm and sensual like him. Sahara's hand brushed a display of sarongs in blue and white bold patterns hanging near the staircase with absent fondness as he and Gecko ghosted to the landing. Sahara nodded to indicate he'd go up first, and Gecko pulled a face. The guy was an adrenaline junkie.

Heart beating, Sahara tested each tread as delicately as he could as he headed for the second floor.

Suddenly a light switched on.

"NOT in your wildest dreams did you think it was me. I'm not unkind to animals, as you saw with your stray kitty. Not until I had to be, anyway, but that was an act of pragmatism, Lotus," Rudy said.

He was tugging Seth down the alley, past his own shop… toward the parking lot at the end of the block.

Perspiration stood out on Seth's forehead as they reached it. *Screaming inside.*

Eyes on Rudy, he managed at last to lift his wallet free of his back pocket. It fell with a thump, loud to Seth's ears. He sagged against the larger man, trying to cover the telltale sound.

"Tsk. You don't handle your medication that well," Rudy noted, smiling. "I gave you just the right amount for your height and weight." He put another little kiss on Seth's mouth, and Seth gagged.

"Don't do that!" Rudy growled, flashing an elbow into Seth's gut.

Seth wheezed, tears running hot down his cheeks.

"We both know you're a whore," Rudy noted, cocking his head to study Seth dispassionately. "I never would have figured, a guy as ordinary looking as you. Never even liked other guys, but that shit you write about…." Rudy shrugged. "Now you better behave like the whore you are, or I'll get mad." His voice was hard, angry whenever he said the word "whore."

Rudy had a black Ford flatbed truck with a tarp over the back. Seth stared at it in horror, wavering back and forth on his feet. Rudy opened the tarp and dropped the bumper before climbing on. He yanked Seth's arm, bringing him to the edge.

"Nooo," Seth moaned.

Rudy slapped him.

Seth's left eye stung from being caught by Rudy's hand. Dead weight, he let himself fall back. But Rudy was strong, a big man, grinning as he lifted Seth easily into the truck bed.

"Nighty-night," he sang as Seth heard the tarp being zipped closed, and then he was alone in the hot, metallic-smelling, enclosed space.

"JESUS!" Sahara swore, his Kel-Tec 9mm handgun pointing carefully toward the floor.

Gecko was kneeling beside the timer, checking it for wires. "Just turns on the bedside lamp." He pulled out a screwdriver. "I'll check behind the electrical plate. Your guy... he wouldn't have left something like this on, seeing as he was, uh, maybe staying somewhere else?"

A flash of interested brown eyes, and then Gecko ducked his head, concentrating. Like magic, the plastic plate fell out as he checked for any sign of tampering.

Sahara shook his head. "No. He didn't know he was going to stay with me. I sort of... persuaded him."

Gecko quirked an eyebrow. "Mmmm."

"And his friend gathered up his stuff, so I don't think she would have known to switch something like this on." Ice feathered down Sahara's spine as he stared at Seth's rumpled bed, at the laptop sitting to one side. "Diversion," he muttered, yanking out his BlackBerry.

Gecko replaced the plate and was on his feet, crowding close to Sahara.

Sahara waited, sickness twisting his guts, and he already fucking knew as he called his home phone number. "Come on, pick up," he growled, hoping he'd be wrong. "Seth, goddamn you, you better be in my living room right now!"

When his message clicked on, Sahara swallowed thickly. He held Gecko's eyes.

"Someone wanted you here," Gecko said in a conversational tone. "Someone wanted to separate you from your friend, get to him. Where would he have gone?"

Sahara headed for the stairs at a run. "I took Jared's car, so he'd be on foot. Probably cursing my name all the way between my place and the shop. Fuck!"

But even as he and Gecko unlocked the front door and raced onto the sidewalk, he knew it was too late. He scanned pedestrians, saw storefronts closing up shop, walked past a leather shop, a shop with piñatas dangling from the overhanging roof, a vegetable and fruit stall, and a coffee shop, and that was the rest of the block.

But no Seth.

"OKAY," Officer Martinez said, rubbing the back of his neck as he paced Seth's store while Sahara watched, arms folded. Gecko was huddled in a corner, reading a *yaoi* manga he'd discovered in Seth's home office while the other two men talked. "So you're saying someone broke in here, although there is no real sign, other than a timer that could have been something Seth used." He raised his hand when Sahara opened his mouth. "Just hang on. So last time you saw Seth was in your place."

Sahara nodded, throat tight. *Keep it together, man.* "I, uh, ordered him to stay put."

"Well, that was certainly effective," Martinez noted.

Sahara rubbed his eyes.

"Hey, man, I think he gets that now," Gecko interrupted.

Martinez blew out a sigh. "Sorry," he said shortly. "Look, I'm just frustrated. We can't officially do anything until the standard amount of time has passed. And Sahara, listen to me...." Martinez squeezed Sahara's shoulder, getting into his space.

On autopilot, Sahara stepped back.

Martinez stared at him and then muttered something that sounded like *ouch* under his breath. "You just met this guy Seth. I mean, how well do you really know him?"

"I know him," Sahara insisted.

"No, you *think* you know him. Everyone has secrets," Martinez noted. He looked around the shop. "I should escort you guys out."

"Come on, don't be a dick," Gecko said. "Seth's friend told you over the phone she'd okayed us being here. Uh...." He cleared his throat. "And she let us in."

"Uh-huh." Martinez's dark eyes glinted.

"Someone had to see something. Or he would have left some sign. He's smart," Sahara whispered. "He's very smart."

Gecko dropped the manga. "Let's go take another look," he said.

Martinez sighed. "I'll wait here until Seth's friend Karen shows to lock up."

Sahara was already opening the front door, a heavy brass cowbell from India adding a *dong* sound.

"Sahara," Martinez called. "Are you really sure you know this guy?"

Sahara closed the door softly behind him, scanning the people walking by.

"Most businesses are closed, but I'll hit the newsstand, the café," Gecko offered. "I've got that picture you photocopied from his home office."

"I'll take the alley that runs behind the shops."

"Would he habitually use that?" Gecko raised a reddish brow.

"No," Sahara said. He cleared his throat, because his voice was hoarse. "Not habitually."

SAHARA stood in the alley outside Seth's shop, closing his eyes, trying to imagine what he'd do if he was Seth's stalker. A ball like tangled chains knotted in his chest, but he breathed past it. Seth needed him to focus.

Okay, first thing was, the guy would have to be close by. He'd have to know Seth's habits. To do that, it would make the most sense to work in the area, to avoid being too conspicuous. So Seth might even know his stalker.

Sahara thought of Seth's kindness, and his throat tightened. He'd probably just said something once to this person and—

He cut off the speculation.

Focus.

Sahara looked up and down the alley, seeing the location of Dumpsters, the doors that led outside from the other stores… and the parking lot just down from Seth's shop. Pricked by instinct, he headed in that direction.

Seth's stalker had to know Seth was staying with Sahara. So he'd lured Sahara up here, probably figuring correctly the ex-SEAL would make Seth wait behind…. but yeah, he had to know Seth, know that he wouldn't stay tamely and wait.

His heart gave a kick when he spotted a leather wallet lying open on the asphalt between the alley and parked cars.

Seth's.

He picked it up, seeing Seth's driver's license, staring at his photo, his brown eyes, his soft curly hair, and then looking beyond at the parked vehicles.

Seth had left him a message.

Chapter Thirteen

SETH knew for sure two things would happen if he stayed in the truck.

First, he would throw up, and although his body needed to do that, he wasn't sure he'd be able to stop once he started. The drug, along with the rough passage they were making and the hot, stifling air inside the truck bed, all combined to make it hard to think through the red pounding behind his eyes.

He could feel every bruise Rudy had put on his body. His upper lip was still seeping blood from Rudy's kiss, which brought his groping thoughts to the second thing he knew: if he let Rudy take him wherever they were headed, he was going to be raped.

He squeezed his eyes shut. He'd begun to hope it would be Sahara who would be his first, Sahara he'd lie under, his hands smoothing over his back, enjoying the gentle dominance that was so much a part of his warrior.

His eyes stung as he thought of Sahara. Capable, soft-spoken, authoritative—which both turned Seth on and pissed him off, depending on the situation—and beautiful. His untamed sand-and-wind-tangled hair, the light blond stubble on his face, the electric blue eyes, and that signature pendant sliding over the hard chest between his nipples....

Even more appealing was the part of Sahara that spent hours working on his dreamcatchers. Seth had so many questions he wanted to ask him about the process, because like any of the artisans he bought work from on his travels, he was interested in what Sahara put into making them.

A tiny smile touched his lips when he thought what Sahara would say if Seth dared to characterize him as an "artisan." The man would be appalled.

I'll be damned if I let Rudy touch me again, Seth growled to himself.

His head smacked against the metal bed as the vehicle traversed what felt like another deep pothole, and Seth bit his tongue, bringing himself back to the present. He had been working on one corner of the tarp, his fingers slightly more nimble as time went on and the drug presumably wore off a little. If he could get it free....

They bounced around some more, and Seth's body was airborne before slamming to the floor of the truck again. A dry streambed? They also seemed to be slowing down. Nearing Rudy's destination?

Shit.

Seth scratched at the tarp, tugging, groping desperately for purchase... and then he had the corner free. Hard, late sun spiked into his eyes, so he squinted. He could see scrub and desert and a dirt road with rising dust behind them. They hit another gully, but this time it helped him because it put his weight into tearing free more of the tarp.

The truck slowed, and Seth gripped the side, leaning over, seeing the big wheel jogging up and down, and before he could *think* about what he was doing and how insane it was, he let himself fall.

"MR. CHALMERS saw Seth when he was closing up shop," Gecko told Officer Martinez and Sahara. He was helping put boxes of fruit and vegetables into the elderly man's shop, his biceps bulging. After a moment, Sahara joined him. "He remembers because it was the last time he also saw his helper today, Rudy Delacourt. He was supposed to do this, pack away all this stuff."

Sahara's eyes narrowed. "Bingo."

Gecko nodded. "Yeah, I figured. He's close to where Seth had his shop, so he could have kept an eye on him and he would have known the parking lot where you found Seth's wallet." He dusted off his hands. "I told the old man he might want to put out an advertisement for someone to replace his worker. And I also found something else."

Sahara and Martinez followed Gecko into the alley between the grocery and the path behind the shops. Next to a Dumpster, he pointed to the cracked asphalt, and Officer Martinez knelt, swearing as he took out a pen to nudge Gecko's find. "We don't know it belongs to Rudy Delacourt. All right, come on, I know, but I'm just saying this is circumstantial." He bent closer to examine the tufts of artificial hair.

"Mr. Chalmers was very helpful. He gave me copies of Rudy's resume and the stuff he filled out when he came to work for him," Gecko continued, pulling some photocopied sheets of paper out of his back pocket.

"I'm betting it's as fake as his facial hair," Sahara said. "But it's a start." His BlackBerry buzzed, and he instantly pulled it out of his pocket. "It's Karen. She texted me that she's still not heard from Seth." His jaw tightened. "She's worried."

Gecko's brown eyes were sober. "She should be."

SETH was face-to-plant with a bushy ocotillo. He rolled into the fetal position, his shoulder throbbing from taking the force of his dive. He strained to listen, but thankfully only caught the fading squeaks and grunts of the truck leaving the vicinity.

For now, Rudy didn't seem to know his captive had escaped.

He forced himself to sit up, cradling the hand he'd used to break his fall to his chest. It was crusted with pebbles and blood and grit. He didn't think it was broken, but the shoulder it was attached to hurt like hell whenever he shifted it.

He sat there, recovering, just breathing, and scanned his surroundings. He couldn't make out any sign of houses or fences or a major highway or anything. Just big round boulders, stalks of upright cactus, and scrub. He wasn't sure of his direction. There were purple slopes of hills but no signs of palms, where there might be water and habitation.

The sun was going down.

Painfully, he tried to get back to his feet.

Moving his shoulder nearly made him black out.

He made it on the third try.

BACK in Seth's shop, Sahara pulled Karen into his arms, using a bit of his T-shirt to wipe her streaming eyes. She covered them after a moment, struggling to compose herself.

Her tears seemed to catch at something in his chest, like a dragnet catching flotsam. He waited patiently because he knew Seth would want her taken care of.

"Why didn't he tell me someone was stalking him? I'm his best friend, for Christ's sake! I thought the rock thing was just... kids, you know? If I'd known, I would have insisted he come stay with me and my husband in our guest room or something. Oh, God!"

"He couldn't stay with you forever, Karen. This is not your fault," Sahara said gently.

She skewered him with a look. "It's not your fault either, Sahara."

"Ah...." He looked over at Gecko, who shrugged.

"I mean, you probably invited him to stay with you because you had a feeling about this stalker thing, right?"

"Partly." Sahara didn't want to talk about the other reasons. He figured Karen could guess.

"He is a stubborn man. He's so unassuming sometimes. Even I underestimate his determination."

"I wasn't thinking." Sahara rubbed his eyes. "I just figured he'd understand me. Stay out of harm's way."

Karen shook her head. "This is the only home he's ever had. He was a foster kid, and I know he survived by keeping his thoughts to himself and being obedient at face value, but he's not like that inside."

Sahara looked around the shop, seeing yarn with vivid rainbow colors that didn't quite compute for him but caught his gaze nevertheless. Scarlets, pinks, amber yellows... and turquoise and yellow-greens.

And there was pottery scattered around, kind of lopsided in construction to his inexperienced eye, but he figured Seth would call it "organic" or something. He'd picked a piece up, and it had felt really light and good in his hands.

"He's passionate," Sahara said. "I underestimated him too."

"So you know he's not going to just let someone h-hurt him." She covered her eyes again.

He had been pushing the thought away for hours. "No, he won't."

Martinez met his eyes over Karen's head. "Call me if you hear anything from Seth, and if you find something out, I expect to be informed."

"Uh-huh," Sahara said, which wasn't exactly a yes.

Martinez grimaced. "As soon as we can make it official, I'll do as much as I can." He turned away, passing Gecko, who had resumed reading his manga, slouching against a display of felting wools colored with natural dyes.

"Karen, I want to stay here with Gecko and look through Seth's stuff. I know he doesn't have any family, so is that all right with you?" Sahara asked.

Karen was rubbing her arms as if chilled. After a moment she nodded. "I'm going to head home now, but I'll be back to…. I'll open the shop tomorrow."

Sahara squeezed her shoulder, and then he let her out, watching as she walked over to her car. When she was safely inside, he locked the shop door and turned to face Gecko, whose brown eyes snapped up to his face.

"Martinez said every man has secrets," Sahara began quietly.

"If we want to profile Seth's stalker, we have to know why Seth was targeted in the first place." Gecko closed the manga and straightened. He was shorter than Sahara but a really lethal guy, as sharp as a fishing knife.

"I brought my own laptop, but maybe you can go through Seth's…." Sahara cleared his throat. He hated to do this, but as the hours passed and darkness fell, it was getting harder and harder not to picture Rudy hurting Seth. He shook his head. No. Seth was shy, sweet, but the man who had built this store out of nothing, had made it flower and thrive, was not a man who would give up.

Seth would take care of himself. He had to. Because if he didn't, there was nothing Sahara could do.

AS HE walked gingerly toward the sloping purple foothills that were an inky mark below star shine, Seth found himself thinking of the artisans he'd met on his last trip to India, men who chipped out wood blocks into intricate designs that had been used for centuries to print on fabric. He knew that life wasn't easy for those workers, and he admired them.

Then there was the woman's co-op where he purchased Turkish carpets for his customers. Many of the weavers were widows with children. He was happy to do what he could to help their families, and their products were beautiful.

He pictured his favorite design, Mountain Flowers, a red carpet with seven different varieties of flowers represented. It always reminded him of the beautiful mosaic work in Topkapi Palace in Istanbul. It would be perfect for Sahara's main living space. He gritted his teeth, shivering a little from the chill that had come with night, and promised himself that he'd be home soon, very soon, and he'd give the carpet he had rolled up in his storage room to Sahara.

Maybe they'd even make love on it.

He paused for a moment, wavering on his feet, trying to grasp what his original train of thought had been. He still felt groggy from the drug. Artisans.... The point was that some of the people he'd met on his travels had endured earthquakes, war, lost their homes and become refugees, and yet still, they'd kept on going. Somehow he would do the same.

After he resumed walking, he stumbled on some loose rock and froze when something shifted nearby, his shoulders falling only when he identified it as a desert turtle, moving away from him at a sedate pace.

He swallowed, his head banging, one arm tucked close to his chest since his shoulder continued to throb painfully.

He had to keep going. If he could find a house or a highway, he could somehow get word to Sahara. He blinked, surprised that his first thought was that *Sahara* would want to help him and not Karen, his best friend. After all, he barely knew the man. He knew Sahara liked Lotus's erotic writings, but this was real life.

Why did he feel like he could count on him?

HOURS later, Sahara took a break from sifting information on his laptop, sitting on Seth's bed as he stretched his arms above his shoulders. He'd been looking into as much as he could find of Rudy Delacourt's life, enough to know that such a person did not really exist. According to his employer, he'd shown up looking for a job about four months ago. He'd asked to take a lower wage and be paid in cash.

He looked over at Gecko, who was munching on some stuff he'd found in Seth's pantry. Seaweed chips. Yuck. His new boyfriend had some strange tastes. Yet, remembering the saffron rice pudding he'd never gotten to enjoy, Sahara hoped he'd get another chance.

Gecko was watching him, brown eyes sober. Sahara tensed, getting a feeling that his buddy knew something that Sahara didn't.

Seeing the abandoned *yaoi* manga sitting beside Gecko where he had staked out Seth's chaise lounge, Sahara raised a brow. "All that time we served together, I never figured we had something in common."

Gecko shrugged. "It's nice you found someone, I guess," he said. "You know how it is in our line of work. If I... had a partner, he wouldn't be informed if I was KIA. He'd have to find out secondhand or some shit."

Sahara nodded. "Okay," he said. "Now tell me what you don't want to tell me."

Gecko sighed. "Right, hope this won't spell true romance biting the dust." At Sahara's glare, he continued. "Well, I think I found a reason why Rudy Delacourt might have fixated on a mild-mannered shopkeeper."

Sahara's heartbeat picked up. Secrets.... So Martinez had been right.

He cleared his throat. It was stupid to care that Seth had been keeping things from him. They'd just met. "Tell me."

"Ever hear of a blog written by someone called 'Lotus'?"

DOWNSTAIRS in Seth's shop, where he'd first met him not so long ago, Sahara paced restlessly, remembering the shattered glass, the charged atmosphere of that initial encounter, how shocked Seth had been by his appearance.

Now he could see why.

He'd actually possessed blown-up pictures of Seth in the nude from his blog, and he'd never made the connection. Seth, of course, had to have known, since Sahara hadn't been using an online pseudonym.

He looked around the space, at the old-fashioned cash register, at the pictures of field workers in India and Egypt picking cotton. At the brass and silver hand-hammered jewelry and Tibetan singing bowls under glass. He expected Seth any moment to show up and share where each piece had come from and why it was special.

Christ, he hoped Seth was okay. He better be okay! He better be somewhere safe, away from Rudy, or Sahara would tan his round, firm, luscious butt.

He squeezed his eyes shut. "Be okay, Seth," he whispered.

Time to go back upstairs, read Seth's e-mails as Lotus. Maybe the fucker who had kidnapped Seth had left some clue there.... Of course, he'd probably find Sahara's comments from Lotus's blog. That is, if Seth had thought enough of them to keep them.

Maybe it was only Sahara who had stored every fragment of correspondence they'd ever shared.

He swallowed and rubbed his eyes before putting his hand on the railing. What did it mean, that Seth had been Lotus all this time and he'd never told Sahara?

Other than that Sahara had sure been a fool.

Chapter Fourteen

SETH woke from a fitful sleep curled in the fetal position. His body shuddered on autopilot, cold even in his sleep. He licked cracked lips, making the upper one that Rudy had split bleed anew. He sat up, head still thumping, and scanned the horizon as the sun rose, gold and pink with tall cactuses in silhouette. Were those palm trees in the distance?

His heart picked up, though it looked a hell of a long way from where he was lying.

Seth managed to get to his knees and used his arms gingerly to brace himself back to his feet, enduring the pain from his shoulder, which had stiffened up.

After a moment, he started walking.

"SAHARA…?"

Sahara blinked his eyes, staring up at Karen's concerned face. He was lying on top of Seth's bed, an afghan he couldn't remember putting over himself tangled around his hips. He guessed rough, tough Gecko had tucked him in when he'd finally conked out.

"Any word?" he rasped. He was still dressed in the same clothes as the day before, his holster and gun resting on the pillow beside him, Seth's laptop open and on sleep mode where it rested on the wrinkled bedding.

Karen's eyes were puffy and swollen. She shook her head. "I was hoping you might have found something."

"Seth has to help us find him," Sahara told her, figuring she deserved the truth. "In the meantime, do you remember Rudy ever hanging around the shop or asking questions about Seth?"

Karen chewed her lip. "A few months back, Rudy did come in here. Seth was off on a buying trip, so I didn't think much of it. He kept me company for most of an afternoon. He was so interested in Seth's stock, I thought maybe he was angling for another part-time job."

"Uh hmmm." Coffee. He needed some, and not that Swiss water decaf stuff that Seth kept in his kitchen. Sahara rubbed his unshaven jaw, seeing that the chaise lounge was deserted. Sometime after he'd fallen asleep, Gecko had disappeared.

"Your friend wanted me to tell you he'd be back soon with seafood wraps and fresh coffee."

"Thank Christ," Sahara whispered, and Karen gave a very small smile.

Sahara found himself reaching out for her hand. She took it. "You should use Seth's shower, maybe borrow his clothes. I know... he wouldn't mind." She swallowed.

"About the only thing of his that would fit me is one of those sexy little sarongs," Sahara rumbled. "And if I bent over too far, I'd moon the world." He closed his eyes, picturing Seth wearing one as he had the first time they'd met. Damn, he really wanted to get the chance to live out a fantasy of making love to him while he wore it.

"Those are sexy?" Her smile was more natural. "Sorry. He's a bit like a young brother, so I don't see him, ah, the way you do."

"I hope not," Sahara said, quirking a brow.

Her eyes sobered. She whispered, "Do you think he's all right?"

"I have to believe he found a way to take care of himself," Sahara said.

"Okay," she said. From downstairs, Sahara caught the *dong* of the Indian cowbell—Gecko was back.

"You took the pictures of Seth. The ones on his blog," Sahara said in an undertone, not wanting Gecko to overhear.

Karen flushed. "Seth finally told you about...?"

Sahara's jaw ticked.

"He didn't." Karen looked down at her hands. "You just found out. Shit."

Sahara wanted to demand she tell him why Seth had kept his double life a secret.

"Is this how Rudy found him?" Karen pressed, rubbing her reddened eyes, her face tight. Since Sahara's guts were knotted, he couldn't do more than look at her. "I knew it! I worried about him writing that stuff."

"He didn't know that someone like Rudy...." Sahara shook his head. "Can I ask you something?"

"Um."

"Why doesn't Seth... date?" Date seemed a better euphemism than trick, though Sahara hated the idea of Seth casually hooking up, no matter how often he himself had resorted to it, needing to burn out his need in someone's body.

Karen sighed. "He had to live his life so much inside himself. I think his writing and his passion for textiles are where he feels safe. From what little he told me, when he first hit the clubs he was underage."

Sahara's stomach twisted. "Shit."

"No, he didn't get hurt, not exactly. But for some reason he was left with the impression that he's not very attractive, kind of a wallflower."

"Hmmm," Sahara said, mulling. Then he shoved back his hair impatiently, changing the topic to something slightly less intimate as Gecko entered the bedroom. The redhead nodded politely to Karen before placing Sahara's hot food and coffee on the bed beside him. "When Rudy was here, did he by any chance ever have access to Seth's living space upstairs?"

"Oh, dear, I never thought—"

"Karen, you couldn't know," Sahara consoled. "But any information about that asshole may help Seth. Right now we don't know enough about who Rudy really is to trace him."

"Yes, Rudy did ask to use the restroom, and the only one in the building is Seth's, just at the top of the stairs. I was busy with customers, so…."

Sahara nodded, picturing it. Rudy Delacourt, or whatever his real name was, had come to Seth's shop when he was not here, deliberately casing out Seth's living space. It was seriously creepy.

"He fixated on him months ago. He had this planned, but something set him off, because he might have easily missed his shot with Seth yesterday."

Gecko put in, blunt as ever, "It was you, Sahara. You coming to Seth's rescue, suddenly being in his life, tipped the balance."

Sahara nodded, unable to speak.

"Take your own words to heart, Sahara; this is not your fault," Karen admonished, squeezing his shoulder. "Now I have to open the shop. Seth would want…. We were going to design the look for holiday gift-giving."

Gecko finished off his herb tea. The guy never drank anything with caffeine. He always said life got him high enough. "I'll help you if you tell me what you need doing," he offered.

Karen nodded, looking from Gecko to Sahara. "Seth's lucky to have met you."

"Haven't really had the pleasure yet," Gecko said, following Karen from Seth's bedroom.

Sahara looked around Seth's space, seeing a pillow and Buddha with some crystals in one corner. He knew enough from Jared to recognize a meditation altar. Shit, Seth should have hooked up with Jared, they had so much in common. Except that Jared was deeply in love with his boyfriend Toby, and it would have killed Sahara if Seth had been dating one of his best friends.

He wanted him for himself.

He guessed he should take that shower. He didn't need a mirror to know he looked like hell.

When his BlackBerry buzzed, he snatched it from the side of the bed.

SETH stared at a few dozen mailboxes standing clustered, leaning together like mushrooms sprouting in the middle of nowhere. Overhead, a running shoe dangled from a power line that ran off down an old paved road. Palms speared up high above him, their tufts of leaves moving in the endless breeze.

Civilization, of a kind.

He even picked up the distant sound of an approaching vehicle.

Seth was never sure later what made him lower himself next to the bank under the palms, but seconds later, he made out a dusty flatbed black truck.

Rudy.

Heart pounding, his hand clenched into scaly bark.

Rudy was out there, searching for him.

He cringed back to the earth as the truck slowed by the mailboxes, almost as if the vehicle possessed a preternatural sense of where its prey could be found.

Seth knew if Rudy had somehow spotted him, he couldn't run far. He was too weak. He could only hide and hope he hadn't been seen.

The truck idled, as if indecisive of what route to take next. Finally, it did a U-turn, heading back the way it had come.

Seth was afraid to raise his head and follow its passage, as if any movement on his part would summon it back, but then he cursed himself as brief clarity opened through the fog; he should have looked at the license plate!

He must have dozed off, because the next thing he was aware of was the sound of another approaching vehicle. He tensed until he recognized it didn't have the deep rumble of Rudy's truck. He looked up to see an older sedan pause and a woman with long dark hair get out and approach the mailboxes.

"H-hey!" He got to his feet, trying to flag her down.

She stared at him, no doubt taking in his torn clothing, the blood and dirt crusting his hair and face. She backed toward her car.

"Please," Seth whispered. He cleared his throat and in a stronger voice asked, "Me puedes ayudar, por favor?"

SETH had his arms wrapped around himself when a familiar blue DeSoto drove up to the oasis with the mailboxes. He locked eyes with Sahara through the windshield until he had to look away, his own stinging.

Karen barreled from the car and almost tackled him.

"*Uh!*"

"Oh, shit!" She let him go, hand covering her mouth. "I'm sorry, did I hurt you?"

"I'm okay," Seth said, seeing her eyes widen as she took in his bruises. He'd gotten a look at himself in the driver's mirror belonging to the woman who had let him use her phone. He knew it looked pretty bad.

"Oh, my God! Did Rudy...?" Her eyes filled with tears. "I'll kill him!"

"I'd rather you were never within a hundred yards of him." Seth crushed her close, not caring if it hurt this time. "And, um, no."

Karen clung to him, and over her head, he saw Sahara watching, hands in the pockets of his jeans as he leaned against the DeSoto. He was unshaven, his hair wild around his face, wearing the same T-shirt as the last time Seth had seen him.

"He didn't hurt me," Seth repeated in a louder voice.

Sahara's jaw worked as he lowered his smoky sunglasses and stared pointedly at the bruising that Seth knew covered his face, the blood still smeared from Rudy's brutal kiss.

"I'll be damned," Sahara said softly, and Seth could feel the flash of his anger, as hot as the sun directly overhead.

"We'll take you to the hospital, sweetie," Karen was saying. She was still crying, and Seth was at a loss as to how to make her stop. He'd told her he was okay.

"I really don't need to—"

"You're going," Sahara gritted out. He took off his sunglasses and put them in the collar of his T-shirt before approaching Seth, as if to take a closer look.

Seth took a step back.

His eyes widened. It had been instinctive, he hadn't been thinking, still groggy from the hangover from the drug combined with no food and water, and Rudy was a big man and Sahara also was a big man....

Sahara looked away, his jaw tight.

"Sahara put on a full-scale investigation, looking for you," Karen chided gently, pulling away to touch Seth's arm. Her touch was careful, as if she was afraid of hurting him, and Seth appreciated it. He was glad he wasn't nude, or she'd probably faint from all the color currently blossoming on his body.

Sahara was looking at him again, and abruptly Seth did feel naked, as if the other man could see every bruise.

"Thank you," he said.

"There's no need to thank me," Sahara grunted. "It was my job."

Seth frowned. "Your job?"

"There's a small hospital not so far from here; we'll take you there."

"But I told you—"

"I know what you said." Sahara glowered at him. "I also know what I see."

Seth shut his mouth, outnumbered. He knew Karen wouldn't relax until he'd been checked out, though all he wanted was to go home, shower, crawl into his bed, and curl up into the fetal position.

And just stay there like that for a very long time.

But then something chilly poked the lower part of his spine, where he still ached from taking a dive out of Rudy's truck. Rudy knew where he lived. Rudy had not given up. Rudy would come looking for him.

Looking into Sahara's eyes, he could see the other man knew it too. His mouth was a flat, grim line, his blue eyes full of lightning.

But what hurt Seth more than his aching body was when Sahara backed away carefully from him, as if afraid of spooking him again, as Karen insisted on walking him back to the car.

"YOU showered," Sahara noted in a low tone as he pulled aside the curtain that separated Seth from the rest of the tiny ward.

They'd been at the hospital for a mere three hours. Seth had been examined pretty fast, maybe because he looked so bad. He felt like his very bones were aching. He just wanted to go home.

Wearing only a small hospital towel, Seth nodded as he watched Sahara close the curtain again. "The doctor let me use the one the staff uses." He was very conscious of Sahara examining him as he reached for the loose scrubs that had been dug up for him to wear since his own clothing was a torn-up mess. "He was pretty good to me."

"He didn't seem to make you uncomfortable," Sahara agreed, looking down at his shoes.

"Sahara—"

"Stop," Sahara commanded.

Seth froze at the soft word, resentment pebbling his skin, but also grief, and shame, and a tiny lick of fear. He couldn't look at Sahara, but he felt him approach.

"I want to see you." Sahara's voice was gentle.

"Sahara…." He looked up then, swallowing thickly.

"I want to see what he did to you." Sahara waited on Seth, as if wary of moving too fast and scaring him. Seth hated that it was a legitimate concern on his part.

Chapter Fifteen

SETH didn't resist when Sahara reached out for the towel around his waist and tugged it so it fell to the floor. He didn't cover his sex, though he did feel a distant desire to do so, but it was muffled by the feeling that… that he belonged to this man.

"Good. Good boy," Sahara praised. He studied Seth, expressionless as he took in the scrapes, the huge swollen lump on his shoulder where he'd taken the force of impact from diving out of Rudy's truck, the imprint of fingers on his left arm.

"The doctor says I'm okay," Seth repeated as Sahara circled him. Despite the state he was in, he felt a bit like a pleasure slave the man was considering buying. He tried to suppress the thought, something like his fantasies, but his cock stiffened a little.

"I knew you would find some way to take care of yourself." Sahara's breath touched the back of Seth's neck, warm and intimate. Seth shivered, and not in fear. "I knew it, Seth."

"You knew more than I did," Seth said wryly. He caught his breath when Sahara's hands cupped his shoulders, very carefully, and then smoothed down his arms. "Sahara…."

"You're very strong, very passionate," Sahara went on.

Seth tilted his head in silent invitation, and a second later, Sahara's warm lips and rough, growing beard touched his neck.

"I don't feel strong right now," Seth confessed, and his eyes stung again. He hated that he seemed so easily to be on the verge of tears.

"You will, I promise." Sahara nuzzled him. "I promised to help you with your confidence, didn't I? Who better than an ex-SEAL?"

Seth felt a smile touch his lips. "It feels like a hundred years ago you said that. Can we…." He turned, Sahara setting him free easily, as if knowing Seth needed that right now. "Can we get back to where we were?"

Sahara pushed a lock of hair behind Seth's ear. "No, Seth."

Seth dropped his head, not wanting to hear more. Not right now.

"What happened to you, you're going to have to process it."

"I know. I just don't want to," Seth said.

Sahara cupped his cheek, and Seth pushed his face into the touch. As long as the big man moved slowly, Seth was okay. "I don't blame you," Sahara said. "I still haven't dealt with some shit that happened to me."

"The scars on your back," Seth said. He had somehow moved closer to Sahara, lured by his sensuous tenderness. He was suddenly in his arms, not crushed tight, but held loosely, so the part of his brain that was still afraid would know he could easily break free.

"Yep," Sahara said. "Other than the doctors, you're almost the only one I can bear to let see them." He raised his brows, and amusement briefly lightened his eyes, like sunlight hitting deep water.

Seth studied Sahara, appreciating his honesty about his vulnerability. It made it easier for Seth, knowing his badass new friend understood. "I'm acting foolishly."

"I don't know what that means," Sahara rumbled, slowly stroking Seth's hair. Seth sensed things under Sahara's calm surface, angry things, possessive things, but not things directed at Seth. He was grateful, since he just couldn't deal with Sahara's feelings about his abduction right now.

What he needed now, more than anything, was this. Sahara's arms around him. His gentleness.

"You were almost raped," Sahara whispered.

"I know." Seth buried his face against Sahara's neck, gripping the other man hard now.

"It would have killed me."

"Oh, Sahara." Sahara had seemed so removed, so angry when he'd first seen him in the desert oasis. Now Seth saw the heart of him. "He didn't." Seth found it in himself to comfort Sahara. "I wouldn't let him. That belongs to us, right?"

"If you still want it to." Something dark moved through Sahara's eyes, but Seth was too worn out, too fragile, to ask him what was wrong.

He settled for nodding. "Just… not for a little while."

"I'm not going anywhere. I can wait."

Seth cocked his head at Sahara as the other man picked up the scrubs and handed him the pants. He was hard from Sahara's proximity, but he was grateful Sahara hadn't pushed it, though he had felt the swollen imprint of Sahara against him when they'd hugged. He just felt all wrong. Bruised. Soiled. Not sexy, despite the autopilot of his body's response to Sahara. "Can I ask you something?"

Sahara waited, folding his arms as Seth tugged on the scrubs shirt. Seth took that as consent. "What did you mean by saying it was your job to find me? Did Karen hire you or something?"

"I went out of my fucking mind looking for you because someone hired me?" Sahara looked exasperated. "No, that's not what I meant."

"Um… I'm guessing my theory isn't correct."

Sahara turned away. "I'll let you finish getting dressed."

"Sahara, wait!" Seth reached for Sahara's arm, just grazing it timidly before he let his hand fall. Sahara looked over his shoulder, his windblown brown-blond hair in his reddened eyes. "I just want to understand. Help me to get it, okay?"

Sahara's gaze was on Seth's bare feet, avoiding his quizzical look. "It's my job to look after you because you're mine," he outlined.

"Oh," Seth managed in a breathy voice.

"You dressed yet?" Sahara cocked a brow.

"Yes." Seth nodded.

"Well, come on then."

But when Sahara made to leave the room, Seth took his arm and let his hand slide down so his fingers wedded to Sahara's.

Sahara glanced at their meshed hands and then at Seth, who was smiling slightly.

He did not pull his hand free.

"Hey, guys!" A huffing Officer Martinez appeared at the open door into the ward. "Glad I found you. Seth, I need to talk to you, get a report on what happened. I already have the doctor sending all the photographs he took as evidence and... *whoa.*"

Seth colored at the way Martinez was staring at him, at the lurid bruises, at his mouth, which looked smudged and puffy after Rudy's brutal kiss.

"You all right?" Martinez asked.

"No," growled Sahara.

"Yes," Seth said. He shook Sahara's hand, still gripping his. The bigger man wouldn't let go.

"Your friend Karen said she'd get some food from the cafeteria. And... here she is," Martinez said.

Karen appeared with a large tray with just about everything Seth imagined they carried for lunch. Sandwiches, soup, coffee, milk, juice, an orange and a banana, and tiramisu for dessert. His throat tightened at the last, remembering Sahara's cake that night over at his floating home.

"Karen, I can't possibly—" Seth began. He swallowed around a bone-dry throat. Martinez was the last man he wanted to talk to right now, and he wasn't sure he could eat while doing it, even though he was feeling lightheaded from hunger.

"Come on," Sahara said. "Just take it one step at a time. Karen needs to eat too, since I don't think either of us ate much the last twenty-four."

Karen gave Seth a tired smile, and he felt a surge of irrational guilt for worrying her. "No, I can see that," he said. "Karen, you can have the dessert."

"I made a big sale this morning, so I figure I've earned at least half," she said.

"What did you sell?" He caught Sahara's amused glance but couldn't help it that the avid shopkeeper in him wanted to know.

"The gothic bed with bedding," Karen said smugly.

"Wow. Uh... well, we'll talk about it later."

"And Gecko helped me with the holiday displays," Karen went on, sharing Seth's pleasure.

Seth sat down with his friends in a small sitting area with tables, gratefully getting off his feet. His whole body ached. "Gecko?"

"Sahara's friend," Karen said. "He helped him search the neighborhood for you."

"Oh." Sahara was sitting so close to Seth that Seth could feel his body heat.

"Which reminds me...." Sahara pulled something out of his back pocket and handed it to Seth. Seth took it, smiling with his relief. "I was dreading getting a new driver's license."

Martinez cleared his throat, looking from Sahara to Seth, and Seth sensed again the man's disappointment that Sahara seemed to prefer Seth. "I need to know everything you can tell me about Rudy while it's fresh in your mind, Seth," he said, taking out a notebook.

Seth nodded, closing his eyes. Maybe if he pretended this was a story, he could distance himself. "When he drugged me, it was some kind of sharp thing that pierced my palm." Seth rubbed the hand in question, feeling the swollen place where the needle had gone in.

Sahara frowned, looking at Martinez.

Martinez nodded. "Sounds almost like a professional M.O. Very slick."

Seth swallowed. "Professional?"

"Mmmm," Sahara said. "It's a good way to take a mark out of a crowd. No muss, no fuss. Guy looks drunk, and you're just his pal, helping him out."

"My God, I heard some rumor that Rudy had been in South America, and I assumed it was some kind of military thing," Karen spoke up. "The story went that he had some kind of breakdown as a result of his service."

"I heard the same story," Seth agreed.

"I'll be checking into that," Martinez said.

"Me too," Sahara said. He was texting something on his BlackBerry. Seth wondered if it was directed at the mysterious Gecko.

"After he took me, he called me a whore," Seth continued. "And more stuff along that line."

Sahara's jaw was tight. "Like the word on your shop window?"

"Yes," Seth said. He cleared his throat. "Listen, I didn't make the connection until yesterday when Rudy explained himself, but um, it may be that he found me through a hobby of mine."

"Hobby." Martinez's eyes gleamed. "You mean the fact you're Lotus, the hottest gay erotic blogger in San Diego?"

Seth gulped, wide eyes on Sahara's face, which was impassive. "Yes."

THE drive back to the city was slow, groggy with late-afternoon sunshine and a kind of charged tension that felt to Seth like waiting for a long, unpredictable fuse to go off. They hit traffic, which further slowed their journey, weaving in and out of commuters until they finally headed down toward the sun on the water and Sahara's home.

Seth didn't argue about their destination. He ached for his home, but Rudy knew where he lived, knew how to break in without leaving a sign. Sahara figured he'd cased it and somehow found a way to bypass the alarm system.

Seth got out of the DeSoto and hugged Karen, seeing that her car was parked in a nearby space.

"Don't come to work tomorrow, or you'll scare away holiday shoppers; it's not Halloween," Karen quipped.

"Nice," Seth said.

"Honest." She shrugged, taking out her keys. "And don't go anywhere without that man of yours."

"He's not mine." Seth gave Sahara a nervous look, seeing he had folded his arms and was leaning against the car with the air of a man prepared to wait a very long time.

"I think he is." She blew out a breath. "I also think you hurt him."

"Yeah." Seth sighed. He kissed Karen's cheek. "Tell your husband hi for me."

"He'll be happy to hear it. He spent a lot of last night rubbing my back since I couldn't sleep," she confessed, tears sparkling again in her weary eyes.

"I'm sorry."

"It's not your fault." Karen headed back to her car, and after she pulled out, there was nothing for it but to turn to Sahara.

Seth stared into his blue eyes, as vivid as the woven beads catching the day's falling sun, and he wondered, what now?

NOW was saffron rice pudding.

Seth lazed on Sahara's brown sofa and watched the other man gather the ingredients and then begin cooking the rice. He was lethargic, feeling weirdly out of time and space—he'd begun the day, after all, curled into a ball in the middle of the desert.

"You were a long time in the shower," Sahara noted.

"That a problem?" Seth felt like digging his claws into Sahara. He had no idea why, but it felt like coming home.

"You know it wasn't, minx."

"Minx. I've never been a minx before."

"Oh yeah, you have."

Remembering the blog, Seth cleared his throat. "I think I like it."

"So after I add the spices, what now?" Sahara asked.

"Cover it to simmer, but keep checking it and stirring occasionally," Seth advised.

"Not good with waiting." Sahara nevertheless seemed willing to follow Seth's directions. "I always want to move on to what's next."

"Thanks for getting my clothes, my stuff," Seth sighed. His eyes kept closing.

"You don't have to go back there until you're ready."

"But Rudy...."

"He's still out there. We'll have to deal with him." Sahara lifted the lid on the pot and stirred.

"Right." Seth squeezed his eyes shut. He knew they'd have to do more than that; they'd have to talk, but he had no idea what to say to Sahara. He'd lied to him by omission. Would he be forgiven?

He must have fallen asleep, waiting on the rice pudding. He knew he was dreaming, could hear his own heartbeat drumming like percussion. He dreamed he was in Sahara's home, arranging furniture. He kept moving it around, over and over and over again, but he couldn't make it perfect somehow. He couldn't get back to who he'd been before Rudy had taken him. Scared him. A chair, a table, only rested briefly in one place, but Seth kept trying.

Finally, in his dream, Sahara walked into the room, wearing only a towel. His hair was slicked back, smooth and wet, leaving his face looking sober.

"I don't know why I'm doing this," Seth said. "Why am I doing this?" But he did know. He was trying to find his home again.

"Stop." Sahara touched his shoulder, and Seth turned to him, seeing in his eyes that he wasn't expected to do anything, be anything... but maybe himself. But how was that good enough?

"Seth," Sahara whispered, pulling him closer for a kiss. "Seth, when you look at me that way, I feel like I've been hit by a baseball bat or something."

Seth parted his lips for Sahara's tongue, needing it like comfort, like tenderness, like Sahara's taste. Sahara's hands ran over his shoulders and then down to the edge of his T-shirt. He raised it slowly, skimming his fingers over Seth's lower belly, just above his belt.

Seth shuddered hard, on the verge of coming just from that gentle tease of a touch.

But when he opened his eyes again, it was Rudy touching him.

"*Uh!*" He woke up with sweat pooled on his chest, his heart galloping.

Scrubbing his cheeks, he took in his surroundings, fighting his body's need to cry. The kitchen was dim now, the pot off the oven. He could smell rice pudding. He wondered if Sahara had burned it or made it into glue without his help.

Seth put his head against his knees.

He flinched when he heard the creak of the hanging chair. Shit. He'd thought he was alone.

"It wasn't so bad. I ate half of it for supper," Sahara said calmly.

Seth gave a choked laugh. "Yeah?" After a moment, he looked up, seeing Sahara's shadowed face. The moon hung swollen and heavy over the water. It was late, and yet the other man was still awake, as if watching over him.

A long time passed then, while Seth fretted about whether or not he should say anything, and there was so much unsaid, and he was sorry.

Sahara didn't speak, just swung back and forth in the chair, and slowly Seth's muscles unknotted into something less than too-tight macramé.

Seth cleared his throat. "Show me how to make a dreamcatcher again?" he finally asked softly.

Sahara climbed to his feet, and Seth knew if he only went into his arms, for a moment he'd feel like he was home.

"Sure," Sahara said.

Chapter Sixteen

SETH got out of the DeSoto, looking back over his shoulder at Sahara, who followed him.

"What *is* this place?" he asked as Sahara reached into the car and pulled out the duffle bag he'd prodded Seth to pack that morning.

"A safe place," Sahara said. He looked like he would have been satisfied sharing only that succinct explanation, but Seth raised a brow at him. "Um. It belongs to a client of mine in the bodyguard gig. He's become a friend."

At first, when they'd driven up a long road to a house that commanded an impressive view of the cliffs and ocean below, Seth had thought the architecture was typical Spanish, white stucco and red tiles on the roof, but he'd noticed the sloping lines had undulated oddly as they got closer to a gateway husbanded between cactus, palms, and some unusual-looking pine trees.

Now he could see the distinctly Asian design. The cut-out white windows that resembled Chinese brocade, the little cedar table with a bonsai gracing the center. More rooflines went on like infinity.

Sahara ushered him inside the open doorway, and he paused in wonder, looking at a floating pavilion. White water lilies bloomed under the hot sunshine. He and Sahara walked under a cool colonnade, providing respite from the heat.

Seth paused to touch a writhing rock-like sculpture with holes and curves.

"Limestone imported from Lake Tai in Suzhou," Sahara said. "Mr. Chan had it brought over."

"This place… I feel like I'm visiting the Forbidden City." Seth put a hand on a red column, looking through rich, polished fretwork at a mountain of rock capped with a small, open garden folly and a roof like curving branches.

"It's modeled after a classical scholar's garden and pavilions," Sahara said. "Mr. Chan used to invite me over for tea when he was in town."

"Why bring me here?" This was the heart of what was between them, as they reached the heart of this unusual house on a floating garden.

Sahara swallowed and looked away. "This place has security twenty-four-seven. You won't see the guards that often, since it's discreetly wired, but I'll sleep better knowing you're here. It's a fortress, Seth."

Seth blinked. "You'll sleep better."

They hadn't slept together since his abduction. He'd been uncomfortable subjecting Sahara to his nightmares, so he'd slept in Sahara's bed while Sahara insisted on sleeping on the couch in his great room.

"Sahara, I wasn't aware you slept much at all. Whenever I'm awake, you always seem to be, if you aren't prowling around outside your house."

"You're not getting better," Sahara said. Then he swore. "Seth, that's not an accusation! Shit, your bruises are still so scary Karen won't let you in the shop."

"I know." Seth shrugged. He both dreaded going back to work and missed it horribly. He just felt so vulnerable when he thought of being there again, the home Rudy had taken away from him.

Sahara cleared his throat. "I also noticed you've stopped writing on your laptop."

"If you mean blogging as Lotus, Sahara, I can't—"

"Do I look like a moron to you?" Sahara pulled a hand through his beach bum brown-blond hair, his blue eyes fixed on Seth's face.

Seth reached out and brushed the vivid beads Sahara wore around his neck like a talisman. He wondered what kind of nightmare had probably woken the other man in the middle of the night to create something so beautiful.

But he knew enough about nightmares now, how personal they were, how things that other people couldn't understand could make you cry, could shatter you, so he didn't ask.

"That part of me is what brought Rudy into my life."

"Rudy is just like the weather, Seth," Sahara said, reaching out as if to cup Seth's tense shoulder. At the last moment, he dropped his hand. He'd been doing that a lot, pulling back from touching. They both had. "He just happens, and you have to deal with it."

"I don't feel very sexy." He hated that Sahara was afraid of touching him, like he had back when he'd cupped Seth's cock, made him come, but he understood. Sahara was a gentle man under the rough-voiced orders. If Seth hadn't seen under his crust before, he knew it now after being held night after night in the aftermath of his fucking nightmares.

"We'll see what we can do about that," Sahara said, clearing his throat. "Making you feel sexy, I mean." But he still didn't reach out.

Seth wanted to be touched. He was afraid to be touched.

In an even softer tone, he confessed, "I don't want you to leave me alone here."

"Tough," Sahara said, but his eyes weren't saying that. His eyes were sorry.

"Sahara, you're not thinking. Who will run my shop? Karen can only do so much."

Sahara chewed his bottom lip. "Uh, I am. And Gecko. And Karen."

"*What?*"

"Thanks for the vote of confidence," Sahara said dryly.

Seth rubbed the back of his neck. "I just want some customers when I get back."

Sahara grimaced. "It's just stuff. How hard can it be?"

Seth crossed his arms. "You are so going to regret saying that."

"Probably," Sahara agreed. He finally did reach out, brushing Seth's hair out of his eyes. "Will you write to me while you're here at Mr. Chan's? I'd... like that."

"I, uh...." He wasn't sure he could. As Lotus, he'd been safely anonymous. As Seth, he was a virgin burdened with bruises and a reserve he just couldn't seem to climb over, even when his body was screaming to be plastered against Sahara's taller one, chest to chest, hard cock to hard cock. He wanted to put his lips to Sahara's shoulder and bite down, leave a mark.

"Seth, hello?" Sahara waved a hand in front of Seth's face, and he flushed, knocking it aside.

"Present, kinda," Seth said. He put his hands in his pockets. "So where do I sleep?"

"Wherever you want. The open water pavilion is kind of cool," Sahara said, taking Seth's arm to guide him there. Somehow, like it always did when Sahara touched him, his hand ended up nestled in Sahara's larger one, feeling a callused thumb brushing over his. The sensation made him shiver, almost as if Sahara had stroked his cock. Oh yeah, he had it bad. He just wished he wasn't even more messed up than usual so he could do something about it.

"It might be a little exposed." Seth would have loved to have stayed there... with Sahara. He wasn't sure about on his own. But how did he communicate that? He couldn't just blurt it out, could he? He wasn't even sure how to seduce Sahara. Lotus would know, but Lotus was a fantasy. If Seth wanted Sahara, he was going to have to figure it out for real.

Okay, he thought, so give it some thought. He just wasn't ready now. He felt ugly and marked wearing Rudy's bruises, but Sahara actually seemed to want him. He had to believe that, because unless he had a huge Boy Scout complex, this taking him to Mr. Chan's was going to a lot of trouble for him.

And he meant to work Seth's store?

As they entered the floating pagoda-like structure, pushing aside breezy white canvas curtains, Seth wondered how that would go. He couldn't wait to hear about Sahara's first day in retail.

"Oh, my...." It was Spartan, letting the architecture and the garden sing, but it was artfully arranged. Two large bronze cranes undulated near one open window. There was one table for tea done with fretwork and then plain, white, padded benches that looked out at different views. Seth could see how they could easily double as beds.

"It's kind of like camping out in an exotic tent," Sahara said, watching Seth as he touched a large copper samovar and tiny, ornate, glass teacups before moving on to look at the rich turquoise and brown mosaics that studded the inner walls like jewelry.

Seth remembered his favorite fantasy, of Sahara as a pasha and Seth as his favorite. He swallowed, suddenly conscious of his breath pumping in his lungs, of the feel of the wind touching him through the gaps in the curtains, of the splash of water from the falls, of his hardness, so painfully hard, so he wanted to fall to his knees and wrap his legs around Sahara's sturdy leg and hump him while Sahara combed his hair, encouraging him....

Whoa.

"You like it, don't you?" Sahara sounded pleased. "That look on your face reminds me of the Seth I first met," he said, and Seth swallowed. Since the first night he'd had the nightmare and groped to put together a dreamcatcher, he hadn't felt like that Seth.

It seemed Sahara was determined to bring him back.

Just then, Seth's BlackBerry chirped, and he noticed Sahara's eyes widen in response at the loudness of the signal. He flushed. "I set it awhile back for e-mails and, uh...." Seth didn't want to spell it out that he'd had it fixed so if Sahara Blue replied to Lotus's blog, he'd be instantly informed. Way to appear pathetically needy, even if it was the truth.

"It's probably Karen. She had a lot to tell me about holiday promotions," Sahara said, looking more apprehensive than if he were facing an armored tank. Yep, he was clearly meant for the retail life.

"Mmmm," Seth commented absently, taking it out and checking his messages. He was not prepared for the wave of cold, sweaty fear that ran through him when he saw what was waiting.

"Seth?" Sahara crowded Seth all of a sudden, but now Seth didn't mind, now he needed him the way he did in the early hours of the night when Sahara held him and Seth clung to him until his tears dried and his heart stopped pounding.

"It's *him*," Seth said. "It's Rudy."

Sahara looked at the picture Rudy had sent Seth. Seth figured his attacker must have taken it with his phone sometime in the alley before he hustled Seth into the truck bed. Seth remembered he'd been dazed then, his ears still ringing from the punishment of Rudy's fists.

Feeling weirdly removed, as if it wasn't himself he was looking at, he noted the blood on his mashed upper lip, his glazed eyes, and wondered what the hell Rudy saw in a guy who could barely even stand on his feet; but then Seth wasn't a psycho, so he was probably missing something.

He was shaking. He was shaking and he didn't want Sahara to know because he hadn't slept in four days and Gecko could only spell him at watch some nights. Seth knew that was why he'd brought him here to Mr. Chan's fortress; he didn't want to let Seth out of his sight, but he needed him safe.

"Jesus!" Sahara rumbled. His face was white under his healthy beachcomber's tan. His eyes blazed blue fire like the Swarovski crystal beads of his pendant. His hands tightened on Seth's shoulders, painfully tight, until Seth made a small sound because he was still sore there, and he hated that he made that sound because Sahara stumbled away, not holding him, comforting him, the way he'd gotten used to.

Instead, Sahara was breathing hard as he stared out at the glittering water that had felt so serene only seconds ago. "I won't," he said softly.

Seth went to him, instinctively knowing Sahara needed him. He wrapped his arms around him, Sahara's back to his chest. "What?" Seth asked.

"I won't let him hurt you." Sahara broke free to turn to face Seth. "Do you know what it was like, the night and day when he took you? Do you fucking know what it was like?" There were tears and thunder in Sahara's voice. He'd always been so gentle, so in control, but hell, had he been feeling this way all the time he patiently tended to Seth's fears?

"I'm sorry, I never thought...." Seth reached out and cupped Sahara's cheek. He couldn't believe this beautiful man was almost in tears over him.

Sahara gave a laugh with no humor in it. "No, you have no idea you've been fucking tying my guts into knots since I first saw you. Do you think I bring every man home I rescue from a broken window, Seth? I don't bring anyone home. But I had to with you."

"So you don't rescue shopkeepers from vandals often?"

"I took one look at you and thought 'He's meant to be mine'," Sahara continued as if Seth hadn't interrupted. "Like Adam's rib or something. Skin and bone, it felt like you were just... mine."

"I want to believe that," Seth said. In his head, he was listening. But years of feeling like he was nothing.... Tears pricked his eyes.

"I don't care what you believe, not now. Now I just want you to know that he will never hurt you again." Sahara stroked Seth's cheeks, still neon with orange and green marks. "I'd let him kill me first."

Chapter Seventeen

"SAHARA," Seth breathed, his eyes tightly closed, tracing Sahara's face with his hands, the prominent bones, the hollows around his eyes that Seth had seen darken with lack of sleep.

Sahara's tongue gave a long, slow lick inside his mouth, sliding against his own tongue in a way that made Seth shiver. "Oh, God! Oh, my God!" Seth's head fell back as Sahara continued kissing him, this time his neck, warm, moist, so he shuddered at the sensation.

He couldn't stop himself; he took one of Sahara's hands and pressed it over his erection. He might not know how to seduce the more experienced man, but he could demonstrate his effect on Seth's body.

"You like that, hmmm?" Sahara's tongue was in his ear now, making circles that made Seth's breath hitch.

"Yes, I am very susceptible to your charms," Seth admitted.

"Are you?" Sahara's voice was amused. He pulled back, looking into Seth's eyes. "It's kind of weird making love to Lotus."

Seth blinked. "It is?"

Sahara nodded. "The shit you wrote... I'm just a man, Seth."

"I admit, at first I saw you as larger than life, like someone I could never have." He put up his hand when Sahara opened his mouth. "I'm working on seeing that as just, uh, the lack of confidence we've talked about, but saying it isn't as easy as *feeling* it." He cleared his throat. "Sahara, you're my first boyfriend."

Sahara leaned his forehead against Seth's. "Why didn't you visit clubs?"

"I was miserable whenever I tried," Seth admitted. "I lied about my age and hit a few places, but the first man who talked to me…. I think he knew I was too young."

"Thank God," Sahara growled. "What about in school?"

"It was like being at home. I just locked down. I knew one day I'd have my own business, my own apartment."

"It says a lot about you that you made that happen," Sahara noted. "I admire determination. But why not apply that to dating?"

"I couldn't imagine it, someone for me. But I could imagine fantasy scenarios."

"Safe," Sahara said, nodding. "It may surprise you, but I am not really great at the scene either."

Seth raised a brow in disbelief. "Why not?"

"I can't ease up, talk to someone." Color scorched Sahara's cheeks. "I'm kind of a barbarian dragging his prey to the cave when it comes to my, uh, encounters."

Seth smiled. "I can totally see that."

"I want to be that barbarian with you, Seth." Sahara kissed him again, and Seth locked his arms around his neck, pushing his aroused body against Sahara's. Ohhhh. It was so wonderful, the brush of an erection against his own, the long, muscled warmth of Sahara. "I want to claim you."

"Yes…." His voice was hoarse. "I'm yours to claim." Oh, this was better than any of his fantasies. This was real, the beard burn against his cheeks, the sweat that slicked the small of his back where Sahara's hand glided before pushing under his pants and briefs to cup one ass cheek, kneading it.

Seth stood on his toes, feeling like wet wallpaper plastered against Sahara. When Sahara stroked him through his clothing again, Seth shuddered. That was good. That was very good.

"Seth, you're still sore...."

"I don't care," he said.

"Need you...." Sahara unzipped him, freeing him so his pants and briefs were piled around his ankles and he was still wearing a T-shirt, which made him feel incongruously more naked than if he was fully undressed.

He jumped when fingers brushed over his dimple, stuttering on sensitive, virgin skin, over and over as Sahara's other hand clenched on his hip. Sahara was suddenly strung tight, his body shaking finely, his breath hot puffs against Seth's cheek.

Seth could see Sahara's focus was on his bare ass, blue eyes heavy-lidded as he pulled away his fingers and then rubbed them over Seth's bottom lip. Seth opened his mouth obediently and sucked on them, moistening them, knowing he was aiding in the penetration of his own body. The thought excited him so much he again wanted to wrap a leg around Sahara and simply hump himself to relief.

"Boy, good boy," Sahara encouraged. The fingers dipped again into Seth's cleft, and Sahara's index finger broached him.

Seth's eyes widened, and he blew out a breath. Oh. That was... oh.

"Hey, you're really tight!" Sweat broke out on Sahara's forehead. "Shit, Seth...."

The finger didn't feel so good. He knew it was supposed to.

"Did you never finger yourself during masturbation?" Sahara asked, pulling back. "Or use a toy inside?"

Seth cleared his throat. This felt far more intimate to talk about than anything he'd done on Lotus's blog. "I started using one after I, ah, met you online."

"You fantasized it was me inside you?" Sahara was continuing to rub, very gently now. It felt better as Seth relaxed and shared with him.

"Yes," Seth admitted. "I needed...."

"You needed some width in there, making it real."

He nodded. He'd positively fucking craved it after talking to Sahara on the blog.

"Did it hurt?"

Seth nodded. "But I liked that."

"You probably put it in too fast." Sahara licked his lips. "Shit, it's hot as fuck to think of you using something inside yourself after talking to me. I always jerked off after you put up a new story. Even when you'd answer one of my comments, I'd have to take myself in hand."

"The last few months, all the stuff I wrote.... It was for *you*, Sahara."

Sahara lowered one sandy brow. "Did you happen to look me up?"

Seth swallowed. "In a pathetic, non-stalker way, yes. You lived so close."

"Why didn't you arrange to meet me? You know I wanted that." Sahara nuzzled him. "Shit, never mind; you thought I wouldn't want you, right?"

"I saw you speaking to Jared. I figured he was your kind of man."

Sahara shook his head, a rueful gleam in his eyes. "We tried once. Disaster."

Seth was avidly curious. "Why?"

"We're both pretty bossy tops. We kept telling each other what to do and banged our heads together at one point. Literally." Sahara grimaced, as if reliving the incident.

"Ouch. Way to ruin a moment." Seth had to smile, also picturing it, though he felt jealous too. Had it been in Sahara's home, his bed? "This had to be before Jared met his boyfriend."

"Mmmm. We decided to leave it. Good thing, too, since Jared was already in deep for Toby. He loved the guy for fucking years before Toby decided to take a walk on the dark side."

"He was a virgin when Jared...?"

Sahara's finger was in a little deeper now, stroking gently. It felt good. Seth stiffened slightly when another was added, but Sahara didn't push too fast, his sleepy eyes riveted on Seth's face as Seth's nostrils flared, perspiration breaking out on his upper lip.

"With men, anyway. They didn't have an easy time of it," Sahara said. "I was relieved for a while that I didn't have a guy, to be honest. Jared seemed miserable sometimes and scary-happy others."

"I've heard that's what love is like," Seth said. He leaned against Sahara now, his hands clenching on his biceps as Sahara continued to probe gently. His finger did a funny little curling motion and Seth felt lightning inside, tightening his balls, making his cock flex so he had to rub it against Sahara's jeans, leaving a little wet spot. "Do I make you miserable, Sahara?"

"Yeah, sometimes."

"Okay." Sahara's answer made him smile.

A third finger went in, and Seth stilled, trying to relax. "Baby, it's like you never had anything up there."

"I'm out of practice, and it's *not* like riding a bike," Seth pointed out.

"I'm afraid to... but I need...." Sahara was trembling. Seth brushed a protective hand down his back before sliding it under his T-shirt, feeling the damp, hot skin. He dared to let his fingers go lower, so they brushed the top of Sahara's briefs.

"Oh, yeah, touch me," Sahara groaned. He pulled away to jerk open his belt and jeans, kicking them off. Next, he tore off his T-shirt. Seth was suddenly confronted by naked, hard-muscled man, tanned except for the swim line of his trunks, but even that skin had a faint golden tinge. Sandy hair tangled around his thick erection.

Seth licked his lips, looking at it. "You aren't.... Wow. I mean, I saw you before, but it wasn't so, uh, noticeable."

"Yeah, uncut. My hippie mom didn't like messing with nature. Do you like it?" Brief vulnerability in his eyes.

"It's beautiful. It makes you look like a barbarian." Seth wanted to get on his knees and lick and suck it.

Sahara seemed to read his want. His eyes darkened. "Oh, yeah. Show me, baby." His hands pushed Seth to the carpeted floor, and Seth rubbed his face against the springy hairs on his thigh.

"Seth, I like you on your knees for me. It's where you belong," Sahara said.

Seth cracked up a little, even though he felt the same sense of rightness. "Not politically correct, Sahara," he murmured, brushing his lips against Sahara's cockhead.

"Oh yeah, Jesus!" Sahara's hands were on his head now, messing up the neatly brushed-out curls. "You want me to be politically correct? Fuck that. I want your ass with my handprint on it. I want my come dribbling down your face." He tilted Seth's face up. "I want to come home and find you naked, on your knees...."

Seth was panting. "Yes, shit!" he agreed. He bent closer to smell Sahara's pubic hair, inhaling the musky aroma. There was no aftershave, no real scents on Sahara except the lemon of his soap. He liked it; it seemed as unapologetic as the mushroom head of his cock. All man. Gently, he pulled back the foreskin, watching precum ooze, then he used his tongue to explore Sahara's slit.

"Christ, look at you doing me! I want to fuck your mouth."

Since he wasn't so sure about his technique, never having done this before, though sometimes he'd sucked his fingers and wondered what it would feel like with a cock in his mouth, Seth was more than willing to open himself for Sahara's use.

Sahara pushed in a little way, his fingers stiffening as Seth licked his taste from his lips. "You hungry for my come?"

"Mmmmm." His mouth was full of Sahara.

"That feels really fucking good. Hum for me, baby." He thrust in a little deeper, and Seth grasped his hips, sucking strongly and then humming and feeling Sahara tremble in reaction. His cock was too thick, too long to take all the way in. He knew he was a little clumsy, but maybe there was no bad way to give a blowjob.

Sahara began to bang his mouth, rutting in and out with more strength. Seth bobbed down and gagged but didn't stop, needing more. His own penis was throbbing white-hot need. It had been a favorite fantasy for so long to take another man in his mouth, to be on his knees, to have his own cock hard and maybe even neglected so that he was forced to come without a touch.

"You remember that intergalactic story you wrote about the recovering slave and the cop who let him sleep in his bed?" Sahara murmured. He was breathing hard, as if his body lived for every brush of Seth's tongue against his cock. Seth was sucking on the foreskin tenderly, and Sahara seemed to really like that.

"Ummm," Seth said.

"The cop was so hot for the sex slave, and then one day he gave in and let the boy suck him off. God! I wanted to hunt you down and make you go down on me, Seth."

Seth pulled away to delicately lick and explore Sahara's length with his tongue and his hand. He'd pictured this over and over again, but this was better than anything he could have imagined. He *loved* Sahara's foreskin. If he'd known how beautiful they were, how fun to see the rim of flesh pull away in excitement, he would have explored them in his stories.

"Have to write this," he said in an absent tone. "Have to write what you taste like, your hand in my hair." He suddenly engulfed Sahara.

"That's it. That's fucking it!" Sahara groaned. "Seth, you better pull back unless you want to…. Baby, I need to come. I want it on your skin or in your mouth, but I need to come *right now*."

"It's okay," Seth reassured him. He pulled Sahara closer with determination. "Aren't I your boy?"

"Oh, yeah…." Sahara began to thrust in and out, his body, his hands rougher with Seth, meaning business. When he climaxed, his cream filled Seth's mouth, spilling out of the corners while Seth's hips jerked convulsively and he also came, came without a touch, came from being on his knees for Sahara.

Chapter Eighteen

SETH opened drowsy eyes. The sun had gotten much lower in the sky since Sahara had claimed his mouth. He licked his lips, still experiencing the faint taste of Sahara on his tongue. It was the first time he'd sucked a man off, so he took some time to savor it. It was not fantasy. It was not something he'd written about as Lotus. It was real.

Sahara rubbed his arm, his long body curled around Seth's protectively on one of the linen-covered benches looking out over the lily pond. A canvas curtain billowed inward, driven by dry winds. It was the warmest December Seth could remember. He felt the prod of a long cock against his cleft. Sahara thrust gently, almost as if it was by reflex.

Seth's barbarian wanted in.

"I took pottery classes a while back," Sahara surprised him by saying.

"Um. I didn't see any in your house," Seth noted drowsily. Pottery? The big, bad Navy ex-SEAL had done pottery. But he knew that if he teased Sahara about it, Sahara'd clam up.

"I have some of my pots in a box in the storage space. Not great shit, but okay. My teacher was Japanese-American, and he tried to teach me all kinds of ways to position my hands to create tea bowls and stuff. I think he moved back to the Pacific Northwest a while back."

Seth thought about why Sahara had brought up this topic. "This was more about regaining dexterity?"

"Mmmm. I also jerked off a lot."

Seth huffed out a laugh.

"I was thinking, maybe… I'd give you the box and you could see if anything in it, I dunno, would be right somewhere in my home. I liked what you did before. I like the new wall color."

"That could work," Seth said. It was funny to be talking about decorating while Sahara nudged him with his penis again, his hand rubbing slow circles over Seth's lower belly. Seth had one knee raised so he could feel the fat head of Sahara's cock making an intimate, wet arc against his skin.

"Shit." Sahara stiffened. He sat up to look into Seth's eyes, his sandy hair tangled over his damp forehead.

"What?"

"Did you even come?"

Color burned Seth's cheeks. He cleared his throat. "No, ah, worries."

"But I…."

"I did just from sucking you."

Sahara's eyes widened as if Seth had done a really great parlor trick. "Really? Wow."

"Is that also a first for you?"

"Yes."

Seth put an arm over his head, stretching. "So did the pottery guy help you with more than making bowls?"

Sahara shrugged, but Seth didn't miss the color that heated his cheeks.

"This thing we have now… I'd rather be the only one moving your clay around." Seth forced himself to hold Sahara's gaze. He would not listen to the voice that questioned if he was hot enough for this man.

"Possessive Seth. I think I like it. I plan on keeping my dance card clear." Sahara put a hand around Seth's throat, like a gentle collar. "I want the same thing from you, Seth."

"Okay."

"Okay what?"

Seth had to smile. Sahara the barbarian was pretty possessive. "No one else."

Seth stroked the big callused hand on his body. He liked it. He liked having a boyfriend. He liked Sahara's smell on him. He liked that they'd both come, that there was a little pool of sweat between Sahara's lower body and his back that hadn't dried.

"I want to see it next time. See you come without a hand on you," Sahara said. He rested his face against Seth's neck so Seth could feel the warm, lazy puffs of breath against his skin.

"Um, you're leaving soon, I assume."

"How'd you guess?"

"Body language."

"Sharp."

"I like studying yours." Seth gave Sahara a kiss. "So?"

"Yeah, I have to meet Gecko. Talk about some stuff."

"Stuff" was probably Rudy.

"Rudy won't stop until he has me again."

"No, Seth, he won't," Sahara admitted. "Gecko's looking into if he had a military history." "What would help find him is me luring him out."

Sahara stiffened.

"Come on, Sahara. You've thought about it. Surely Gecko has brought up the idea? It's only logical, even for us non-law enforcement, non-military background guys." Seth regretted the sudden distance of their bodies and Sahara's tight jaw.

"You bring up that idea when your body is still covered with his bruises? I'll be damned," Sahara growled.

Seth stifled a sigh. His lover was a bodyguard, a protector. He was hardly going to embrace the idea of Seth as bait. "But Officer Martinez suggested—"

"When?"

Seth faced Sahara, and the old Seth, the timid Seth, might have backed down at his eyes, burning like lit gasoline. But he'd sucked him off not so long ago, and Sahara's legs had given a little wobble, and next thing they were both collapsed on one of the banquets.

"At the hospital," Seth said.

"I'll talk to him." Sahara's tone said, *I'll kill him.*

LATER, Seth sat on one of the curvaceous rocks and watched turtles pile up on the sole sunny rock in the middle of the pond. Apparently they had a pecking order that needed frequent revision since only one or two of them basked at a time. Seth enjoyed watching them, and as long as he didn't move, they didn't plop back into the depths of the pool.

John Marsters appeared, the silent head of the bodyguard team that watched over Mr. Chan's vacant house. He was in his mid-fifties, a recent emigrant from Scotland who made the best, the very best Earl Grey tea Seth had ever had.

"How did you know I needed more tea?" Seth asked. He had his arms wrapped around his legs, still feeling the burn of Sahara abruptly shoving on his clothing and leaving.

Damn it, he'd still had stuff to say!

Now Marsters set the tray down, watching Seth through steady gray eyes as he poured frothy milk into a cup.

"Did you use actually use a cappuccino machine to foam that milk?" Seth asked, watching as Marsters poured his tea.

"Trade secret, sir," Marsters said, smiling.

"Hmmm." Seth personally thought that was taking making tea a little too seriously, but it tasted wonderful, soothing and hot.

"Sahara left somewhat abruptly," Marsters noted, sitting on another rock.

Seth sipped, deciding to take the invitation to confide. It was not like he had much experience with relationships. Maybe Marsters could offer some insight. "Yes, we, uh, had an argument."

"It's good he has someone to fight with."

"You've known him a long time?"

"Mmm." Marsters helped himself to some tea, as if he tacitly understood that Seth would be more comfortable if they were both taking it. He reached for some fresh-baked cookies on the tray and passed the plate to Seth, who took one. Seth noticed an unsightly scar on the back of the older man's hand, like something from a knife fight. It was incongruous to take homemade baked goods from a man who looked like a battered fighter.

"How did you meet him?"

"I can't really say," Marsters said, munching on his cookies. "Except it was when he was employed by the Navy."

"Wow," Seth said. "Before he was hurt."

"Yes."

"What was he like?"

Marsters smiled. "In the village where I grew up, that was the kind of question asked by young women about a boy they were curious about."

Seth raised a rueful eyebrow.

"To answer your question, he was cold, very focused."

"Uh-huh." Seth stared at the pond, trying to reconcile that with the man he knew now. "He doesn't seem that way to me. He has always been very protective."

"That is what you fought about, how he wants to protect you?"

Seth nodded.

"I don't think he's that man anymore, except with strangers."

"But I was a stranger not so long ago." Seth had finished his tea. He put down his cup, wondering if it was too soon to call Sahara. He decided it probably was.

Marsters shrugged. "I was instructed to ask if you know how to dance."

Seth blinked. "Huh?"

"Sahara Blue wants to take you to a special club for dancing."

Seth's eyes widened. Sahara had insisted he dig out some tight black jeans and a silk sweater that stretched snugly across his slight chest when he'd been packing to stay here. Was this the reason why? He chewed his lip, thinking about it. "You know, I think I can learn."

SAHARA was not in a good mood when he returned to his floating home. He nodded to Gecko, who was sitting outside on the deck, chilling out in the sun.

"Dude," Gecko said. He studied Sahara's face. "Lovers' quarrel?"

Sahara shrugged before unlocking his door. His cock still had that satisfied *I just had sex* feeling that he wanted to savor since it was so fucking rare. Too bad he was too tense to enjoy it. "Tell me you have good news on how to find this fucker and end him."

Gecko quirked a brow. "You better not let Martinez hear that."

"Martinez has never had a capable and crazy stalker kidnap his ass."

"Seth was hurt pretty badly?" Gecko followed Sahara into his home office, slouching against one wall and crossing his arms. He'd been called in to do exercises in the immediate aftermath of Seth's abduction, so he hadn't yet had a chance to meet him.

"He only escaped because he took a swan dive out of the guy's truck bed into the desert. He's lucky he didn't break his neck or just get fucking lost." Sahara's face tightened. "And Rudy kept hunting. Seth saw him at one point and hid himself."

"Sounds like he has good instincts," Gecko said.

Sahara grunted. "So who is Rudy?"

"You aren't going to be happy."

"I'm already not happy." Sahara's stomach tightened at his friend's expression. Bad, this was bad. But hadn't his instincts been whispering? The way that Rudy had stalked Seth for months, the way he'd gotten into his home, cased out his business, the way he'd taken Seth by surprise, getting him quickly under control. Only Seth's determination and the fact that Rudy had underestimated him had meant he wasn't somewhere now… at Rudy's mercy.

"He is ex-military."

"Shit."

"An ex-Ranger who is also wanted for questioning about the disappearances of two freelance mining engineers he was employed by in South America. They went into the jungle with him and never came back. He went off the grid at that point."

Gecko took out a folded piece of paper from his pocket and handed it to Sahara.

Sahara took it, seeing an old photograph of Rudy.

"His real name is Randolf Maxwell, thirty-seven years of age," Gecko said. He rubbed his eyebrow. "It's rumored that he had a kind of crush on one of those engineers, Sandy Brandon, a young woman from Tacoma, Washington."

Sahara swallowed, feeling sick. "So he got her somewhere isolated, took out the other engineer, and…."

"Likely," Gecko said. "No one's seen Sandy or Michael Thompson, her partner, since. Her parents posted a reward for information, but...."

Sahara shook his head. "No one's going to find her." *And no one would have found Seth, if he hadn't gotten clear.*

"Seth wants to set himself up as bait to draw this guy out."

Gecko raised a brow but didn't speak.

"We'll find another way," Sahara said.

"The apartment Maxwell rented just had the basics, nothing to trace him. It looks like he had a setup for a laptop, but he took it with him to work every day."

"He was ready to take Seth at any time. Close up shop and just take him." Sweat broke out on his forehead at the thought.

"He's out there," Gecko said. "And he's not going to stop."

"...AND I was thinking that it would be nice to have one of those beds made of driftwood to replace the gothic bed we sold off the floor," Karen said, updating Seth over the phone later.

"It's gone now?"

"Yep, customer picked it up at noon."

Seth nodded, picturing his shop. It was frustrating not to be there, to be able to pace and envision what to fill a bed-sized display space with. "Maybe the wooden dining table with some of the hand-screened burnout cushions we just got in?"

"The Persian design?" He could hear Karen moving around in the shop, and a sudden worry struck him.

"Karen, you aren't alone in there, right?"

Karen laughed. "Sahara has one his bodyguard buddies in here all the time we're open."

"Shit." That had to cost a lot. He'd have to bring it up with Sahara. He was perfectly willing to pick up the tab to keep Karen safe.

"At least the guy can move some of the heavy furniture around for me," Karen said. "Okay, I'll do up a display with the Persian cushions."

"And order the driftwood bed." Seth had a sudden idea. "In fact, order two of them."

"Two?"

"Um, I may want one, or, you know, Sahara…."

"Uh-huh." Her tone was amused. "It would look great in his place. Should I get a king?"

Seth flushed, glad she couldn't see him to tease. "Yes, a California king."

"Will do. Boss…."

"Yeah?"

"Try not to fret. I know it's not easy for you to be away from this place, but enjoy your vacation."

Seth sighed. "I'll try, but Karen—"

"I know. You will only stay there so long."

DANCING. He was going dancing.

Seth had found the idea kind of alien at first, but as he brushed a hand over his sweater, which molded to his slight body, he was warming to it more and more. He stared into his own wide eyes, seeing that the bruising wasn't quite as unsightly. Marsters had given him a bit of makeup to cover it up, though he'd been taciturn about why he had something like that on hand. Seth had pictured the older man maybe dolling himself up like a drag queen, but he certainly hadn't shared the idea.

He lifted his arms above his head as if he were on the dance floor, turning, and when he met his gaze again, his heart had picked up.

He had also hardened, so he wet his lips and ran a hand down the front of his jeans. He was going to a club with Sahara, the hottest guy that Seth had ever seen. He knew that tonight was not going to be like those times he'd tried clubs before, when he'd felt too shy, too boring to catch anyone's eye.

The mirror caught Sahara's reflection as he entered the pavilion where Seth was waiting, the same one where, just hours before, Seth had sucked him off. His blue eyes ran over Seth's body as he came up behind him, putting his arms tightly around him. He buried his face in Seth's neck.

"Hey, you all right?" Seth pulled free and turned to study his lover.

"Dandy," Sahara said.

"Uh-huh."

"Tarting up for the mirror?" Sahara cupped his cheek, examining Seth's face. "The bruising looks way better." He narrowed one eye.

"I didn't want to look like someone hit me with a truck. It's not sexy."

"It is when you consider that you had the stuff to get yourself out of a bad situation." Sahara rubbed Seth's arms. "Strong is sexy."

"I'm not used to thinking of myself as strong."

"Okay, let's take a look at that picture." Sahara pushed Seth so he was again facing the mirror. "Foster kid finishes school and then works three jobs to save the money for his first buying trip. He goes over to India and travels a country he in no way can be prepared to experience at nineteen, seeks out artisans of dying crafts...."

"Hey, you've been talking to Karen." Seth covered his eyes in embarrassment. Sahara pulled them gently away so he was forced to hold the other man's steady gaze.

"She likes me, what can I say?"

"She wants to do you, except she's married."

Now Sahara Blue blushed. "She's shit out of luck. I have it bad for a formerly timid shopkeeper who is turning into a handful." His voice was caressing, as were his eyes. "Now, to continue with the biography. You spent two years traveling, selling your work to merchants in LA, New York, Seattle, wherever you landed until you came home to San Diego and opened up your shop. You specialize in sustainable crafts and natural dyes. You've even gone to some villages and helped to start spinning and dyeing for the specialized rainbow knitting yarns you handle."

"Sounds very impressive."

"It is." Sahara leaned his forehead against Seth's. "Speaking of inventory…." He picked up a plastic bag from the floor that Seth had noticed he'd arrived with. Seth peeked inside and nodded with satisfaction. "Your dreamcatchers. Thank you for trusting me with them. Uh, we didn't discuss pricing."

Sahara shrugged, looking uncomfortable. "That's your thing, so you handle it." He cleared his throat. "The one I helped you make is at the top."

It was turquoise, with a dark plum bead in the center, posing as the spider in the web of dreams. Seth had wanted something in a color that reminded him of Sahara's eyes, though he hadn't told the other man that. Yet. Maybe one day. "I'll hang it tonight. Will you…." Seth turned around to fit his smaller body to Sahara's. "Will you help me do that?"

"Sure."

"Okay, then. The dancing… this is about helping me with my confidence. Sahara, I should warn you that usually guys ignore me at clubs."

"Not tonight, they won't. Now let's go dancing."

Chapter Nineteen

THE club that Sahara took him to was one that Seth had imagined many times, but the location was certainly nothing he'd pictured.

"We haven't left Mr. Chan's estate!" Seth exclaimed when Sahara pulled up in front of a large pavilion situated out in the desert night. There were lumps of purple hills and spiky palms and the glitter of a pool, this one more suited for humans to use than turtles.

"I thought since you couldn't go to the party, not safely, then…."

"You'd bring the party to me. But why?" Seth ran a nervous hand over his tight jeans. "Sahara."

"I just pictured you maybe hitting a club when you were a little too young, unsure of yourself, hungry to find the right guy."

Seth's eyes widened. "You've been that guy too?"

"Seth, I'm that guy *all* the time. You think because I can field strip a weapon, that I can fly a plane, navigate a boat through a reef in the dark, skydive from high altitudes, keep my knife up when I'm bleeding and my vision is graying out…. You think because I've done all that, I know how to be smooth at a club and meet—" Sahara swallowed. "—someone like you?"

"Wow, you've done all that stuff?" Seth blinked. But he made himself study Sahara, truly see him. Not be dazzled by the fantasy, by the assumptions he'd made. Sahara wasn't wearing anything special as club clothes, just jeans, white at the seams, that cupped his sex snugly, and a tight black T-shirt. His signature pendant flashed blue fire, catching the eye. He hadn't even put on socks, obviously more comfortable in the black pull-on runners he used for jogging.

"What?" Sahara looked at him. He reached out and smoothed the side of Seth's face, his touch tender.

Unexpectedly, Seth's throat tightened. He cleared it. "Just the way you're dressed."

"I don't really do the club thing," he admitted. "I'm a terrible dancer."

"I doubt anyone would care. They'd look at you and think, look at that *man*. Mmmmm." Seth quirked a rueful brow.

"Yeah, and I act the expected part but after, it's awkward. I don't want to take him home and I don't know what to say, so I just disappear."

Seth reached out and touched Sahara's necklace. "Five hundred beads. I counted," he said when Sahara gave him a surprised look. "It had to be really delicate work. It had to be a really bad night, huh?" Now he could see Sahara more clearly. The dreamcatchers had been his first clue. The night after Seth himself had returned from his own ordeal in the desert was his second. His hands had been shaking so much that night from his nightmare that Sahara had twisted most of the ties of the dreamcatcher they'd made together.

Sahara looked away.

"No, don't do that." Seth caught his face.

Sahara sighed as he faced Seth again. "One night I remembered my buddy Miguel. He was a newlywed, one of my best friends. Maybe I screwed up, and that got him killed."

"Sahara," Seth breathed.

"I don't really know for sure."

"You made this in memory of him?" Seth touched the crystal beads.

Sahara nodded. "I wanted to have a way to always remember him. He loved the ocean, so that's why the color blue. And after I finished making the pendant, I logged on the web and somehow found you."

Seth swallowed.

"You were my Scheherazade, telling me a story every night so I just had to hang on to read it, and after a while, you know, it wasn't so bad." Sahara stared into Seth, and his eyes were the absolute true blue of his pendant.

"THIS location… it's because Rudy is going to be watching the store, or maybe your house," Seth guessed.

"Seth, I don't want you to think about him tonight," Sahara said as he walked Seth into the pavilion. "When he took you, all I could think of was, I wanted to take you dancing."

"I thought you don't dance."

The music was throbbing, a primeval beat. Seth found his excitement picking up as they walked over a white stone bridge and into the large pavilion. There weren't many men there, but whoa… gorgeous men. Seth's eyes widened. "It's like a candy store in here! Who are these guys?"

"Couple from my bodyguard gig. Some musician friends of Jared's and two actors from his soap, I think," Sahara said.

"Hey, guys," Toby greeted them. Sahara he pulled into a slightly tipsy kiss while Jared looked on indulgently. "Thanks for inviting us. Jared went swimming, but I had a really rough day, so…."

"You're sloshed," Sahara noted, not seeming to mind that Toby's arms were around his neck. Seth, on the other hand, wasn't feeling like his old wallflower self. Instead he felt—

He tugged Sahara's arm, pulling him away from Toby. "Dance with me."

Sahara's eyes widened, but he seemed to appreciate this new side to Seth. "Whatever you say, minx."

There was only one other couple on the floor, and they were moving together more like they were slow-humping while standing up than really dancing. Seth couldn't help watching them, and then he shrugged, pushing aside his shyness. If that couple didn't want to be looked at, they'd dance somewhere alone.

Sahara slid a hand up and down his hip. Seth could feel the knob of his erection rubbing against Seth's own hardness. He licked his lips. "I feel like a minx tonight."

"Is that right?" Sahara leaned his forehead against Seth's. "What would Lotus do in a place like this?"

"Lotus...." Seth half closed his eyes. "Lotus would take his clothes off and dance naked with the man he wanted. And while they danced, they'd attract a crowd, and other men would touch him, would want him, until his lover had enough and carried him away... probably over his shoulder."

Sahara's eyes were riveted on his face. Seth soaked up the attention, and *whoa*, had Sahara grown even harder where he was rubbing against Seth's hip?

He laughed, conscious of the gazes of some of the beautiful men in the room on them. It felt good. It felt completely hot, like hands touching their skin.

Suddenly Seth didn't want to just fantasize. He wanted to *live* what he dreamed up. He stopped dancing and stepped back from Sahara, and as the other man stared at him, he pulled off his T-shirt. Up until Rudy had kidnapped him and he'd managed to survive that ordeal, he'd been embarrassed by his slight frame, but when Sahara reached out and grazed his chest with his fingers, he could almost see himself through Sahara's eyes. His skin was silky in contrast to Sahara's roughened fingertips. He was lean and firm and wiry.

He ran his hands up and down his chest, holding Sahara's eyes, smoothing fingers over his nipples, circling his belly button as his hips rocked back and forth, slow.

"Shit." Sahara wiped away some perspiration that had broken out on his upper lip.

Seth laughed again, feeling like he ruled the night.

He reached down and made a teasing motion with his hands over his belt. And then when someone yelled "Go for it, yeah!" he undid the leather and some of the buttons of his jeans.

Sahara wasn't even pretending to dance now. He stood watching Seth as he gyrated his lower body, circling the larger man, running playful hands over Sahara's back, tousling his hair. Sahara's cheeks were stung with color by the time he faced him again.

Other men had come closer, some holding drinks, watching Seth and Sahara with a predatory light. Seth caught glimpses of them when he wasn't staring into Sahara's vivid blue eyes. He traced Sahara's pendant before boldly pinching one of Sahara's nipples through his T-shirt.

"*Uh!*" Sahara gasped, covering Seth's teasing fingers with his palm. He held that hand against him before lifting it and kissing the back of it. Seth felt the graze of Sahara's teeth and shuddered.

After a moment, Seth's hands went to his jeans. He felt hot and wild, like an untamed beast he was daring Sahara to try to control. Still holding his gaze, he undid the rest of the buttons and let the jeans sag below his rump.

He jumped when someone pinched him from behind, whirling around to see who it was. But there were several attractive men standing there, watching him, smiling, and he couldn't guess who had touched his ass.

The jeans he kicked away, and then he was wearing only blue silk briefs, gloving a stiff and unsubtle erection.

He took Sahara's hand and placed it over himself, whimpering when Sahara squeezed him gently, but when his hands went to the edge of the briefs, Sahara pulled him close. "*No*, please."

Seth blinked.

"I want… this"—Sahara stroked him—"for me." His face worked, as if he was struggling with words, and Seth remembered how he'd said he didn't exactly come across as Mr. Smooth when he frequented clubs.

The next instant, Seth got the rest of his fantasy; Sahara lifted him high and then tossed him over his shoulder.

"We're leaving," Sahara growled.

THE finger of moon above them was like an eye in the dark, watching them.

On his feet again in the desert night, Seth breathed in the scented air, aware of the pavilion, a glowing white futuristic construction in the distance, of the gurgle of water from another pond, this one surrounded by patio lounge chairs and a table. "I still have my sneakers on," Seth noted. "Not quite the striptease Lotus would have pulled."

"Lotus didn't have to tread through rough terrain," Sahara said. He cupped Seth's face. "You know what's going to happen?"

Seth nodded, his heart suddenly pounding in his throat. "When Rudy had me, I had to get away, stay alive. I wanted you to be my first."

"You get your wish," Sahara said. He pulled off his own T-shirt and tanned muscle shifted, grooves and hills that Seth wanted to trace with his lips. But it was the snake of one scar that curved around his hip that caught Seth's attention. He dropped to his knees on the pavestones, still warm from the heat of the day, and put his mouth against it.

"Ummmm," Sahara moaned. "Seth, I love it when you're on your knees for me."

Seth smiled against Sahara's skin, loving that only *he* was allowed to touch Sahara's scars. "The dancing was hot. Thank you for that."

Sahara caressed his hair, the vibe that of a master stroking his pet. "You weren't overlooked. If I hadn't been there, you'd have been under a lot of guys tonight, one way or another."

The thought sent a curl of pleasure down Seth's spine. "Why does that give me a wicked thrill?"

"Because you're a bad boy. That underwear is fucking sexy, by the way, the way it gloves your ass."

Seth gave a little wiggle of said ass and then licked Sahara's scar, and the play of Sahara's muscles tensed under his tongue like a vibrating guitar string.

"Don't stop now!" Sahara prodded, raising sandy brows. His face looked stern and serious under the moonlight, but there was a tiny gleam of mischief in his blue eyes. *He was having fun, as Seth was having fun.*

"You shouldn't dare me tonight. I might do anything," Seth said, unbuckling Sahara's belt. He pressed his lips to Sahara's denim-covered erection, worshiping it. "I feel like an acolyte in some kind of pleasure temple that might have existed once."

"Shit, your stories...." Sahara's fingers clenched on Seth's scalp gently. "Play it out. Tell me something that will make me so hot I'll just shove you down and fuck you."

"Oh." Seth's eyes widened. He licked his lips, deciding *yes*, he wanted that. It had gone so well when they'd danced, Sahara playing along with him the way they'd spun out a previous fantasy together. "I am a virgin in the temple. I've been prepared to service men my whole life. I *ache* to do it, to lie open and feel someone thrusting inside me."

"Jesus!" Sahara's hands joined Seth's as they undid his jeans together, Seth punctuating his story with nuzzles and kisses to Sahara's prick.

"But I'm only to be given to a special man, a man who needs my body to heal him." Seth pulled down Sahara's briefs and mouthed the hard cock he unveiled.

"Uhhh, I definitely need to be healed!" Sahara thrust himself so his penis nudged Seth's lips, leaving shiny precum there. Seth licked the taste, looking up at Sahara through heavy eyes.

"Yes, you do. You're a legendary warrior for the empire, but you've become a bit of a recluse so it's decided that I am to be your gift."

"Bring it!" Sahara laughed, and Seth laughed too. Sharing this was like sharing a glass of fizzy champagne. Why had he ever been afraid to be Lotus with Sahara?

"The first time is in the ceremonial temple." Seth tugged down Sahara's jeans and briefs, loving his naked body under the moonlight, so male. Mmmm. His cock, his heavy, hanging balls, his thick thighs and taut stomach and the luxuriant sandy pubic hair. "They prepare me on a stone altar, covering me in oil, and then they bind me, my wrists and ankles. When you arrive, you have some noble idea that maybe you'll refuse this gift, but when you see me, see how I look at you, how I ache for you...."

"I burn," Sahara said.

Chapter Twenty

SAHARA knelt beside Seth, cupping his face. Seth finished toeing off his runners, peeling his underwear down and off. He paused and nuzzled Sahara, like a smaller animal might with a larger, dominant one, taking a moment to study his lover. His large eyes, which were a deep indigo in the moonlight, the line of his mouth, heavy now with desire, his flushed cheeks and the tiny freckles Seth had never noticed on his clear, tanned skin. He brushed a kiss just above where sandy stubble outlined Sahara's lips.

"I burn, Seth," Sahara repeated. "Since the first time I read your words. You have no idea how many sleepless nights you put me through!"

"I know I should say I'm sorry," Seth said, amused.

"Minx. You are not sorry."

Seth sat back on his rear end, taking hold of Sahara's pull-ons and removing them one by one. "I wrote because I was lonely and there were things I needed to express. It was worth it to find you."

Sahara grunted when Seth settled in his lap and then pushed him so he landed on his back on the flagstones. Seth put his hands over Sahara's, his hair swinging against his cheeks as he looked down into startled blue eyes.

Mmmmm. Sahara Blue wore nothing but his signature pendant and a loop of beads around one ankle. His cock prodded the back of Seth's ass. Seth lifted the wrist that had the seashell on the inside of it and kissed it, closing his eyes and savoring this. He was here, nude, under a starlit sky, with the man he'd fantasized about. It was strange how they'd met, almost as if it was fated to happen sooner or later.

"Seth, like this. I want to start it off just like this," Sahara whispered. "Um, as long as it's not too uncomfortable for you."

"Did you bring anything?" When Sahara nodded, Seth lifted his jeans from where they'd abandoned them in a heap and went through his pockets, pulling out lube and some condoms.

"Your new confidence," Sahara said. "It's sexy. I like looking up and seeing you on top of me."

"I guess Rudy did me one favor. When I thought there was a good chance I wasn't going to come back, I decided I was not going to sleep through the rest of my life, settling because I was afraid to take a chance. Dancing tonight, being watched, being wanted; I liked it."

Sahara sat up a little, gripping Seth's hips as Seth's lubed fingers disappeared behind him. His face tightened and then relaxed after a moment. Sahara stared up at him, rapt. "Tell me another story."

"What kind of story?" Seth grunted. He added a second finger to the stretched opening, seeking and finding his gland. Whenever he rubbed it, he made a soft sound until Sahara gripped his ass cheeks tighter in his hands, kneading them.

"Shit, it's hot watching you do that." Sahara's eyelashes dropped. "What do you think might have happened if I hadn't hauled your ass out of the pavilion tonight? And be sure you finish this one—it used to kill me, the way you'd make me wait to see what would happen next online." His voice was slightly accusing.

"My apologies," Seth huffed. Sweat broke out on his upper lip as he added another finger. "Let me see...."

"The way all those guys were watching you. I know what they wanted."

"What did they want?" Seth asked softly. He rocked against Sahara's hard body.

"I imagine they wanted to see me fuck you. Pull you down onto one of the benches by the pool, spread you out, maybe gag you and—"

"Gag me." Seth stroked himself. "Shit."

A little smile curled Sahara's lips. "You'd be kneeling at my feet, your head on my thigh, nude. And maybe you'd mouth me through my jeans until I had enough."

"I could do that!"

"I always wanted to give you what you needed, baby. I wish you'd just come to me a long time ago. I practically dared you to."

Seth cocked his head. "What do you think would have happened if I'd just shown up at your house one night?"

"You'd have been flat on your back in about five minutes!" Sahara said.

Seth grinned. "Is that right, tough guy?"

Sahara's eyes closed as Seth kissed him on the cheek. "I thought it would kill me; you were so sexy, but you were so sad, so insecure. I was afraid to spook you."

Sahara picked up one of the condoms, and Seth shifted his body slightly to the side, giving Sahara access to his erection. He watched the other man fumble with it. Sahara finally got it rolled on the third try. His hands were shaking.

"Nervous?"

"Yeah!" Sahara huffed. "What the fuck! I have no idea why."

"So you want to know what happens next in my story?" He looked into Sahara's eyes as he reached back and gripped Sahara's penis, holding it tall. "Write it with me."

"Oh. Ah!" Sahara's eyes nearly crossed as Seth experimented with sitting on his prick. He'd lift up and then push down. "Oh, Jesus...."

Seth finally found an angle that seemed a little easier. Sahara's fat head broached him. He breathed out, sweating. "It just goes in, right? I mean, it has to fit."

Sahara cleared his throat. "It's just… snug. Uh!"

Seth pushed down further.

"Easy, baby." Sahara caressed Seth's back.

"Why, again, did I think you being well hung was a *good* thing?"

Sahara kept up rubbing Seth's back, as if coaxing Seth to let him in. "If we were back in the pavilion, and we'd been together a while…."

"What?" Seth was wide-eyed. It burned, Sahara slowly penetrating deeper, and somehow the story went with the raw sensation.

"Maybe I'd just spread your legs and let someone else fuck you while I watched," Sahara whispered. "Would you like that, Lotus?"

"Maybe. Uh!" Sahara was lodged so his balls met Seth's ass. The other man was trembling, his face slick with sweat. Seth could see what an effort this was. It hadn't been easy to accommodate Sahara, and now he was trying to be gentle.

Feeling like he was leaping off a cliff and flying for the first time, Seth raised himself and then lowered, thickness lodged deep inside. He was riding cock. He'd dreamt of this moment forever. Too bad they hadn't had time to tie him up, to leave him helpless so Sahara could just take him. "I think now I've done this, I want… oh, shit… to be a slut."

"As long as you're my slut." Sahara's arms went around Seth, and next thing, he managed to wobble onto his feet, somehow keeping Seth impaled. "I can't… I need to fuck you."

"Sahara?"

Seth's back was suddenly against the brick half-wall where a barbeque was embedded to one side. Sahara's muscles bulged as he thrust inside Seth—hard.

"Oh, God!"

"No more nice guy. No more waiting. No more being sensitive." A bead of sweat rolled down Sahara's cheek. His pupils had almost swallowed his irises as he held Seth's gaze. "I just want to fuck you. I don't want to be an understanding boyfriend. I don't want to be patient and sweet. I don't want to talk. I want to *fuck*."

Seth's thighs clenched high around Sahara's thrusting hips. "I need it. I need it," he chanted. Sahara kept shifting, and he wasn't sure why as the brick scraped his back, but then his big cock slammed into Seth's gland and... oh! Oh, shit. "Do me. Do me just like that."

"I'll do you." Sahara held him with one arm as he hammered. The other palm moved over Seth's face, stroking roughly. "You're so hot you could sell it on the street."

"You could sell me," Seth's head knocked once against brick. He didn't care. He just needed to come. Sahara was giving it to him, giving it to him hard, like he needed. "You could tie me down and give it away."

"Fuck, that's hot!" Sahara moved so Seth's body was even higher, so he was squished against hard wall and hard man, taking it. "That's so hot. You're so hot, and you make me crazy! You make me just want to shove it in, no talking, no bullshit—"

Seth arched, his balls drawn up tight, his hand gunning over his cock so he knew it would be sore later, but he didn't care—

"*Fucking hell!*" Sahara shouted, shuddering, his neck corded, his face distorted. "Fuck, you slut, you did this. You needed it and I— fuck!"

Semen hit his face, his chest, as he erupted, screaming. Seth's vision dimmed, as if all his energy rushed through his balls, his cock, primal. He was still huffing, blown to pieces when Sahara's legs gave out and they slid-crashed down the brick, down to the paving stones, and Sahara's forehead was against his, and they were both panting. "Oh. Oh," Seth groaned. His cock shot again, one last pull— sustained—and then he was dry, dead, toes still extended, his throat rough and sore.

THEY curled against the shelter of the wall because the wind picked up, a little chilly against sticky, cooling flesh. Somehow Sahara managed to stagger over to his discarded T-shirt, and he put it over Seth like a blanket, holding him as he shook.

Seth wasn't aware he was crying until Sahara whispered, "I take it back. I'll be a sensitive boyfriend. Sometimes."

Seth choked out a laugh. "I think I'm going to walk funny. Like a gay penguin, maybe."

"You'll be the hottest bird in the neighborhood."

"I didn't know you'd be the one. I didn't know…."

"I am, I was, baby." Sahara kissed him, raising the T-shirt to scrub Seth's damp cheeks. "I'm here."

"I was so scared," Seth said, remembering Rudy. "I feel like there's nothing I can do, like he'll get to me."

"I'd be dead before that happened." Sahara pulled Seth so he was sitting on his lap.

"That's what I'm most afraid of," Seth said.

SAHARA finally rallied them so they stumbled back to the pavilion, which was quiet now but not deserted—from inside, Seth caught the sounds of men having sex. His cock stirred, but his body was heavy and hammered into submission and too sore.

Sahara guided him into the pool, and he shivered, rinsing off. "My only regret about tonight is I wish I'd had your come dribbling down my legs," he said.

"Shit!" Sahara dipped his head back so his sandy hair floated around his face, looking like a water spirit. "The stuff you say."

"Just being honest."

"Your honesty will fucking kill me."

BACK at Mr. Chan's central house, Seth walked the colonnade with Sahara, finding it refreshing, calming, after what they'd experienced. His senses felt scorched, his body grounded by the warm palm against the small of his back, guiding him forward.

"Our cat," Seth said, a little groggy. "I know you told me someone else has her...."

"Don't worry, she's with Karen. Gecko doesn't like cats."

"Really?" Seth giggled. "A big, bad Navy SEAL who's afraid of a kitten."

"Yeah, you be sure to point that out when you meet him. He'll love you for it."

Seth yawned, huge. His jaw cracked, and he almost couldn't stop. "Good, that's good Karen has Lotus."

"Gecko's staking out my place. When I leave tonight, I'll probably watch your store." Sahara yawned. "Stop yawning. Stop it."

"Stay."

"Seth."

"Stay." Seth looked at him. "I love you. I love what we did. I don't know if I love how my ass is feeling right now, but—"

"It'll pass. I can work some cream up there if you're really raw."

"If you put anything in me, you'll want to fuck me."

Sahara shrugged, but he didn't deny it. They reached the little pavilion on the water, the curtains billowing inside, and Seth collapsed on one of the benches, reaching underneath for the drawer where pillows and blankets were kept. He was just doing what he had to, to get all he needed so he could conk out.

But he wanted Sahara to stay.

"I can make you tea," he offered. "There's... tea stuff."

"Just sit there. I know where it is. Let me take care of you, baby." Sahara pulled out a burner and lit it and then put Earl Grey tea leaves in a Japanese metal pot.

"You're not going to foam the milk first?" Seth asked, eyes half shut.

"What? No." Sahara blinked.

"Okay." Seth laughed, finding Sahara's puzzled expression hilariously funny.

"Someone needs their cornflakes." Sahara rooted around and found some of the pastries Marsters had left with the tea. Seth snagged one from him and shoved it in his mouth. "Or possibly a blood transfusion."

"More."

"Crème caramel or brownies?"

"Brownies."

Sahara passed Seth the plate, and Seth inhaled one. "Stay here."

"Okay."

Seth sighed, relaxing against the bench. The blanket was wrapped around him, the tea was steaming, and Sahara wasn't wearing a T-shirt. He appreciated the view of his man as his muscles flexed, and he even liked the scars because he knew normally Sahara would have covered them.

But not from him. He was Sahara's exception to the rule.

When the tea was ready, Sahara added sugar and carefully brought Seth a cup. "I like being pampered," Seth sighed.

But Sahara's gaze was suddenly fixed on the water outside the pavilion. "I didn't...."

"What? My mind-reading antenna is busted for the rest of the night."

"I didn't hurt you, did I? I was kinda—"

"You didn't hurt me. You *wrecked* me."

Sahara's lips turned up as his eyes finally darted up to meet Seth's. Blushing a little at Seth's approving look, he sat down on the stone floor in front of Seth, cross-legged and graceful, as if he assumed a yoga position regularly. Damn, he was beautiful. His hair was a mess from Seth's hands, and his lips were reddened from the crash of their lips.

"So, I just want to know one thing," Seth said, putting aside his tea since he'd finished with it. He was ready to sleep, but one thing nagged at him. Tomorrow he knew if Sahara didn't give him the right answer tonight, it would resurrect the unwelcome ghosts of his insecurity. "Do you... are we going steady now?"

Seth stared into his eyes, and then he did the last thing Seth expected; he unhooked the clasp for his signature pendant and put it around Seth's neck.

"I can't, Sahara! I know what it means to you!" Seth gripped Sahara's wrist.

"You'll just have to keep it safe for me," Sahara said.

Seth's throat tightened. He had his answer. "Okay," he rasped before Sahara pulled him into a gentle kiss. "Okay, I can do that."

Chapter Twenty-One

SETH woke covered in the heaviest blanket he'd ever worn: Sahara Blue.

Seeing his lover was still deeply asleep, he took a moment to study him, sandy lashes, flushed cheeks from sleep, tanned skin, the heavier blondish stubble on his cheeks that rasped gently against Seth's neck with each breath Sahara took.

As if feeling his gaze, Sahara's remarkable eyes opened, and Seth remembered the night before, and the gift of the pendant, the same color blue. He'd always been quiet, unassuming in real life. His fantasies had all been sexual, but this... this was something he'd never imagined for himself. A man who put *him* first.

"I can almost make out the thought bubble above your head," Sahara rumbled. "It's getting heavier and heavier, so it just might pop."

"Yeah, I think I'm on overload," Seth sighed. "This thing with you...."

"Whatever it is." Sahara nuzzled him. "Yeah."

At least he wasn't lost in the woods alone, Seth thought.

Sahara reached down between them, to where Seth was hard. Seth groaned at the touch. "Don't think," Sahara advised softly.

"Ummm, okay." Sahara had them both in hand now, lubricated by precum. Oh, shit. Oh, God. This was definitely the best way to wake up. Ever.

"Fast. Want it fast?" Sahara's hand quickened its pace. Seth arched up, thrusting. "I like it fast. I want to do you slow, baby. I want to do that so much, but now I have you…." Sahara groaned. "I just need to— God, you're so sexy. Your hair is curly. Do you know it's curly?"

Seth laughed, but then—

"Ah, *ah!*" He creamed first in Sahara's grip, but then the other man rutted harder and cried out, teeth biting into Seth's shoulder.

Huffing and dazed, Seth watched as Sahara got up—on the second try—and dipped a clean towel into the pool that surrounded the pavilion. The water was chilly against sensitive, overheated flesh, so he caught his breath, flinching.

"Not used to roughing it?" Sahara teased.

"If you mean eating bugs from logs or some kind of survival deal like you no doubt have mastered, no," Seth said. "On the other hand, I have taught cold water dyeing techniques in villages where firewood is a hard thing to come by."

Sahara frowned, arms tightening around Seth. "Where the hell did you do that?"

Seth bypassed his concern with a kiss. Which was very effective. After sustained sharing until they only parted so they could breathe, Sahara joined him back on the bench. "Maybe we can manage slow now," he muttered, mouth going to one of Seth's nipples and sucking gently so it beaded under his tongue.

Seth gripped Sahara's head, hands making a further wilderness out of his bed hair. "Oh, yes. Yes, I think we need to do slow. Ah, Sahara!"

"You're mine now," Sahara whispered against his skin.

"Better get used to it," Seth finished with a faint grin, remembering when his warrior had first said those words to him.

Of course, he was wearing Sahara's talisman now, so it was a done deal.

"I'LL be damned," Sahara growled later. He scrubbed his eyes before putting on his shades.

Sitting next to him in his borrowed truck, Seth didn't pick up the hook for another argument. All that mattered was that he was here, driving into town with his lover. They'd compromised that Seth would have a quick visit to his store before it opened, after Sahara checked in with Gecko. Sahara was insisting that the SEAL come with them, and Seth didn't ask if they'd be armed. He knew he was lucky just getting to come into town at all.

But like Karen had said, this was his life. And after the night before, when he'd celebrated being a sexy gay man, how could he continue hiding? Rudy was not going away. Seth felt instinctively that he'd have to face the man again.

But right now.... He put his hand on Sahara's muscled thigh, giving it an appreciative squeeze.

"Don't try to get around me, Seth, with your flirty ways," Sahara said gruffly.

"I have 'flirty ways'?" Seth was delighted. He couldn't wait to live that new power. A fantasy scenario popped into his head of himself as some kind of delicate pagan king and Sahara as his stalwart bodyguard. Of course, it would be forbidden for the king to sleep with a common warrior, but Seth would do it. Mmmmm.

"You know you do, minx. You've been driving me crazy for months," Sahara said as they pulled into the wharf parking lot.

"Better be careful, now I got my claws into you."

"No kidding. Want something from one of the food stands?" They hadn't eaten since after the slow second time they'd made love. They'd wound up fighting about Seth coming into town. Only his saying he'd damned well do it without Sahara had made the difference. But he couldn't take sitting around doing nothing at Mr. Chan's serene pavilion another day. Not without checking in at his beloved shop.

"Yeah, that would be great. Seafood wraps and hot coffee?" Seth got out of the truck, intending to accompany Sahara, when Toby suddenly appeared, giving Sahara a kiss on the cheek but then spreading the love by bestowing one on Seth. Seth blushed and Toby laughed, obviously enjoying Seth's shyness.

"Hey, guys!" Toby exclaimed. "I have the *worst* hangover."

"Who is to blame for that?" Sahara asked without sympathy, raising a sandy brow. He was wearing the cool-as-shit smoky sunglasses which Seth found super sexy.

"You sound like Jared," Toby groused. "Too bad you disappeared. It's been a while since I've had two gorgeous men ordering me around."

Seth's eyes widened.

Sahara swallowed, darting a glance at Seth. "Yeah, um."

"Oops," Toby said.

"You've played with Jared and Toby?" Seth asked.

Toby looked upset. "I didn't mean to fuck things up!" he said. "I'm too impulsive sometimes." He looked at Seth, blue eyes contrite. "It was just a bit of safe play, because I know he's not into Jared."

"Hmmm." Seth would have to think about this.

"We found a place for the marbled cushion from your shop. Do you want to see it?" Toby asked. It was transparently an olive branch, and Seth couldn't resist. He could feel Toby's genuine regret that he might have caused problems between Seth and Sahara.

"Okay."

Sahara's lips parted as if he wanted to say something, but after a moment, he sighed. "All right. But stay with Toby. Do *not* go off on your own."

Seth wanted to ask him where he'd go, but he stowed it. He knew Sahara was worried, and he remembered Rudy. His eyes. His cold determination. "I won't," he agreed.

LEAVING Sahara to stand in line for the food, Seth followed Toby down the wharf toward the floating home he shared with Jared. The morning sun flashed red and gold on a beautiful stained glass door with a merman and sailor who resembled the two lovers.

"What's it like, living here with Jared?" Seth asked.

"I gave up my condo about three months after I moved in," Toby said.

"I guess that says it."

"Yeah." Toby scratched his tumbled fair hair. "Look, Seth, I just wanted to say that... that Sahara splashed around with us in the shallow end a couple times when we first got together. I'm a pool guy, so excuse the parallel."

Seth climbed onto the deck of Jared and Toby's home, taking in the gathered driftwood and assorted crystals, sparkling in the sunlight. There was a small Buddha carved from amethyst in one corner that he recognized as an outdoor altar.

"He was lonely and single. But when I first met him, he was also absolutely fucking *obsessed* with a blogger named Lotus."

Seth cleared his throat. "It was mutual."

"Jared is the one who believes in Karma and all that. He'd say you two were fated to meet." Toby held his gaze, his freckled face absolutely earnest. "There is just no way I'd ever do anything to screw up something so important to Sahara, you know? He's... he was there for us, solid, during a very difficult time."

"Thanks," Seth whispered, relaxing. Toby was pretty cute, so that even wearing Sahara's pendant, Seth couldn't help but feel just a little bit insecure. "He's very special."

"He's a hero." Now there was no tentativeness in Toby's voice.

"He still has nightmares."

"He tried to save one of his buddies from that helicopter crash. That's how he got the scars," Toby said. "Jared told me."

Seth's chest tightened. "I had a feeling; he's so protective."

"Seth, I noticed what you were wearing right off." Toby's blue eyes were sober as he gestured toward Sahara's pendant. "All his friends... we know what that means. You're special to him. I know he's gorgeous, but he's been so lonely."

Seth nodded, unable to speak. He was grateful for Toby's sensitivity. He didn't feel insecure now. It was clear Toby wanted Sahara to be happy.

Just then, he noticed a stocky, muscled redhead out on the deck of Sahara's home. He was frowning, hands on his hips. His silent disapproval was obvious as he glowered over at Toby and Seth.

"Gecko," Toby said. "Come on, I'll introduce you. Never mind the cushion, we should probably go over there until Sahara shows up."

Seth nodded, giving in and following Toby. He really hated that his coming into town today had upset Sahara. He wasn't reckless. He'd been to some places in his travels that required sensible precautions, and he well remembered his ordeal with Rudy. He would do whatever he could to—

A huge plume of flame exploded from Sahara's floating home.

Heat, debris blasted out, knocking both him and Toby from their feet. As if he were doing some fantastical kind of cartwheel, Toby rolled right off the wooden pier, splashing into the saltwater.

Clinging to the wooden planks, Seth shielded his eyes and looked up at Sahara's house, seeing a huge black flower of smoke erupting from the center. It was listing against the pier, sinking fast.

"Oh God!"

There was no sign of Gecko.

Coughing, Seth managed to make it to his feet. He crawled to the edge, checking the water desperately for Toby. "Shit, shit!"

A red hoodie floated just beneath the surface; Toby had been wearing it.

Seth dived in, snatching for the hood. He grabbed it, reaching up for the side of the dock. "Ouch!" Burning wood! There was shit everywhere! He heard shouting, caught the thunder of running footsteps.

Familiar tanned hands grasped him, pulling him out of the water in a surge. Seth coughed, still holding a death grip on Toby's clothing. "Help him, Sahara!"

Sahara reached down and also pulled Toby's limp body onto the dock, cradling him. Toby's face was pale and lax; he wasn't breathing. Sahara shifted him closer and opened his mouth, clearing it before he put his mouth against Toby's, breathing life.

Seth had two hands over Toby's heart, pumping. "Come on, Toby! Come on!"

Sahara breathed into him again and again. Each time he pulled up to check, Seth died a little, waiting. Tears seeped down his cheeks, hot against the cold seawater.

Please.

Toby choked, and Sahara held him as he coughed. His eyelashes flickered, but he didn't open his eyes. His forehead was bleeding and there was a shard of wood sticking out of his chest, just below the shoulder.

"Sahara, the paramedics are on their way!" a grizzled man said, kneeling next to Sahara. "They were down here gettin' coffee and wraps at the wharf, thank fuck."

Sahara nodded. He stroked the hair off Toby's face, very gently.

When the gurney appeared, Sahara stepped back, and he and Seth watched as Toby was very carefully moved, the paramedics working over him.

Finally Sahara looked over at the wreckage of his home. Wood, ash, black smoke. Very little was still above the waterline. "Gecko?" he croaked.

"He was… oh, God, I'm sorry, Sahara! Last I saw him, he was on the deck."

Sahara started for his home at a run, and Seth followed. Sahara peered into the water, shoving aside a burning dinghy to get closer.

Suddenly a figure popped up from the surface like a curious water mammal.

Sahara reached out, and Gecko took his hand, climbing onto the dock.

He looked at Sahara's home. "Seemed like a good time to abandon ship." He looked at Seth. "Hey."

AT THE ER, Seth stood with Sahara, waiting. Suddenly Jared appeared from around a corridor, jogging toward them. When he reached them, he gripped Sahara's arm.

"Jare," Sahara said. "He was breathing. I know he was breathing. They rushed him into surgery."

Jared cupped his mouth.

"Have you called his parents?"

Jared nodded. "They're both on their way. They've been distant with Toby since…. But none of that matters now, does it?"

Sahara squeezed his shoulder. "No."

Jared said, "If he dies, I don't want to live."

"Don't think that way. That kid is stubborn, and he loves you. He'll come through for you."

"If he—"

"He was breathing on his own. You'll be lighting healing incense in no time," Sahara said. "Feng shui-ing his fucking hospital room." He leaned closer. "Hold on," he whispered.

Hot tears welled in Seth's eyes as he watched Jared nod. "I have to. His stepfather worries about him a lot. You wouldn't know it but—"

"They're here now, by the entrance. Go talk to them. We'll be here."

Seth watched as Jared walked toward an older couple. The older man reached out and grabbed his arm, and Jared spoke to them.

"My fault," Seth whispered.

"No," Gecko said, appearing with coffee for all three of them. He was sipping his. He had a Band-Aid over one eyebrow; other than that, he appeared in good shape, but his eyes were sober as he looked over at Jared and Toby's parents. "Rudy probably swam over one night, attached something on a timer."

Seth's eyes went to Sahara, who nodded, grim. "It's what I would have done."

"But why?" Seth asked, rubbing his head, which was sore from slamming against the pier. He saw again Sahara's home, burning, sinking. Toby's pale, unconscious face as Sahara dragged him from the water. "Oh God, *why?* I wasn't anywhere near your house. He couldn't know—"

"For me," Sahara said, just as if it didn't bother him at all. "He came for me."

Chapter Twenty-Two

SETH just broached the entrance to the chapel, seeing Jared. He was not sitting in one of the pews. He was front and center, where various religious symbols rested on a block of wood, curled against it on the floor.

He looked up and tensed when he spotted Seth.

Seth raised a palm. "No one's looking for you. Toby's still...."

Jared squeezed his eyes shut and rubbed them tiredly, nodding. He didn't move from where he was sitting. After a moment, Seth joined him, sliding down next to him and putting a tentative hand on his shoulder.

Jared stared at the terrazzo floor.

Seth pulled his knees up and let his head fall back against the wood block.

SAHARA BLUE looked up when Officer Martinez and a man he hadn't met before appeared in the waiting room. He excused himself from Toby's parents and met the two men further down the corridor.

"I'm sorry about your home, Sahara," Officer Martinez sighed. "Sorry about Toby too. Any word?"

Sahara shook his head. "He's on shaky ground."

"Jared must be...."

Sahara's throat tightened. Martinez had been a stand-up guy when Toby and Jared had dealt with someone who tried to destroy the first home they'd made together. "Yeah."

"This is Adam Gregory; he's an investigator with the fire department."

Sahara nodded at the man. "I guess one good thing was, my house sank before it could burn too long and set anything else on fire," he told Martinez with grim humor.

"I'll have to ask you some routine questions about the blast that took it out," Gregory said. He had a shock of white hair and a deeply tanned face. Frank green eyes held Sahara's gaze. "Officer Martinez informed me that there might be another element at play, some kind of harassment?"

Sahara's face tightened. "It goes further than that. Randolf Maxwell, aka Rudy Delacourt. He's wanted for questioning regarding the disappearance of some American freelance engineers in South America. And he has a thing for my boyfriend, Seth Hollis."

"...DAMAGE to his heart. He's in recovery right now, but he might need additional surgery at any time," the doctor warned Jared.

Jared scrubbed his face, and Sahara put an arm around his shoulder as Seth stood behind them. Toby's stepfather wiped his eyes while his mother sat down, as if to absorb the news.

"When can we see him?" Toby's stepfather croaked.

"I'll let you know when that's possible," the doctor promised.

"I need to... I need to get out of here for a moment," Jared whispered.

"I'll go with you," Sahara offered.

Jared shook his head, his pupils blown so he looked shocky. "No, I—"

"I wasn't asking," Sahara said. "Toby would want me to look out for you until he can do it again."

Sahara drove around aimlessly with Jared, not talking, because what the fuck would he say? Jared needed a breather before he went back to the hospital and waited to see if the man he loved would pull through.

"We should go down and see your house," Jared finally said.

Sahara wanted to ask why, but he left it. Jared's eyes were glassy, and he kept smoothing his palms down his jeans, over and over again. Periodically, though it didn't ring, he checked his BlackBerry.

"Toby's parents will call you if anything changes. It's their shift now, Jare, and you know...." Sahara swallowed. "You know this is going to go on a while from what the doctor said."

"I know that. I have to eat. I have to meditate...."

They pulled in at the wharf parking lot, which was less chaotic than it had been hours before. The fire trucks and ambulance were gone. The crowd of bystanders had dissipated. Now it was just the locals, some of whom were already sweeping and gathering up debris, overflowing the Dumpsters.

"Sahara," Jared said. "I'm not sure I can meditate. I can't eat."

"Then don't," Sahara said.

As Sahara and Jared made their way down the pier, their neighbors came out, looking first at Sahara and then not asking Jared how Toby was. Some patted his shoulder as he passed them, others just stood in silent support.

"It's a good place to live," Sahara remarked as they approached what was left of his house.

"Yeah," Jared agreed, still looking out of it. Then his gaze sharpened on Sahara. "Will you rebuild?"

Sahara shook his head. "Not sure what I'll do."

Gecko was at the end of the pier, pushing back goggles and his dripping hair off his forehead. He hefted something, and Sahara's throat tightened on seeing it. "Went in as soon as they were done," he said. "This is all I could find that looked salvageable. Sorry, man."

Sahara took the carved statue of the Balinese lady he'd bought Seth when he'd first slept over. She smiled enigmatically up at him. "No," he said, clearing his throat. "No, this is perfect. Thank you."

BACK at the hospital, there was no change. Jared sat with his head in his hands. Finally he got up, heading for the chapel.

Sahara gripped the little statue in his hands until Seth reached out and took it from him.

"It's a little chipped," Sahara noted. "Scorched on one side. I figure I could sand that off, maybe."

"I'm glad she made it. Sahara… were you able to salvage anything else?" Seth reached out and stroked the wind-driven hair out of Sahara's eyes. He looked exhausted. They all were, but no one could sleep.

Sahara shook his head. "It's a write-off, Seth."

Seth ached, remembering how lovely Sahara's home had been, how they'd just started to work on it for him.

"Guess it was a good thing we didn't have time to invest too much in the decorating thing," Sahara said.

"I want you to come stay with me," Seth said. "You have a home there… I mean, if you want it. If it's not too soon."

"Seth…."

Seth closed his eyes. "Right. Rudy. We can't forget he's out there."

A muscle worked in Sahara's jaw.

"I don't want to go back to Mr. Chan's house. I did that and someone else got hurt. I want to end this." Seth remembered the desert, remembered babbling to Rudy as he dragged him to his truck. "He has to go down."

Sahara blinked, as if he hadn't expected Seth to say something like that. "Okay." Seth saw a kind of lightning move through Sahara's blue eyes.

"Okay? We get him?"

"We definitely get him."

"GECKO went over the shop and your apartment," Sahara said. He closed the pad for the new alarm system he'd installed when Seth had stayed at Mr. Chan's and slouched against the wall, facing Seth, who was going through the receipts of the last few days since he'd been in the shop. He didn't enjoy the bookkeeping part of running a store, but he had to do it and he couldn't rest, any more than Sahara could rest, not while waiting for news on Toby.

"So we should be okay, right? I mean, he doesn't want to kill me. Not right away, anyway."

Sahara's eyes flashed. "No, not right away."

Seth dropped his gaze back to his paperwork. After a moment, Sahara cleared his throat. "I need to do something. Tell me what to do."

Coming from around his old-fashioned till, Seth went to his man and reached up to knead his shoulders. Sahara pulled him close, and Seth nestled his head against the other man's shoulder. "You must be desperate if you're asking me for retail therapy."

"I must be," Sahara concurred. "I'll sweep or... or move shit around. Whatever."

Seth pulled back, studying Sahara and then looking around his shop. "It's about two weeks away now from Christmas. Shit."

Sahara blinked. "It is? But I'm kind of used to, I don't know, tuning it out."

"Your family?"

"Just my mom, and she passed away one winter when I was overseas."

"I'm sorry."

"At least I knew her." Sahara threaded fingers through Seth's hair. "More than what you had." He also looked around the shop. "Karen did a little bit."

"Yeah," Seth agreed. "But...."

"Let's get it ready," Sahara said. "Let's just work on it and get it ready for the holidays."

"So Toby can come see it?" Seth's eyes misted. He laid his head against Sahara's shoulder again, loving the gentle strokes of a big, capable hand up and down his back.

Sahara swallowed. "Yeah, so he can come see it."

"WAX." Sahara blinked as Seth heated white chunks in a double boiler. "This has something to do with the holidays how?"

"I was in France over the holidays one time, and there was this shop. Incredible. It was flowers and chocolates. They decorated everywhere with waxed fruit, branches, dried flowers."

Sahara looked blank. "Uh-huh."

Seth laughed. "Indulge me, big guy. I promise it'll look very holiday."

"And that's all that matters."

"Yep."

IT TOOK some time to dip each chilled flower and fruit. Sahara went down to the fruit stand and bought some pomegranates and some dark plums. "Look like shoes, polished to shine," Sahara noted when they'd finished with the gathered assortment.

Seth had out some old-fashioned cream ware that he'd collected and loved to use in the holiday displays. He mixed in driftwood with the collection, giving it a seaside twist. Sahara watched, though his gaze was often more on Seth than on his creations; Seth knew it was because he'd changed into a sarong. Sahara seemed to like him wearing it. He'd also lent an extra-large one to Sahara, since most of his clothing was gone.

When he was finished, Sahara picked up one waxed rose and placed it behind Seth's ear before kissing him. "I want to go somewhere exotic with you. Somewhere warm. Just… sail away."

Seth flushed a deep red, his chest, his face, at their closeness, at the simmering arousal that never quite went away, smoothing his hands over Sahara's broad bare back. "I'd like that."

"You seem pretty attached to your shop, your home." Sahara raised a brow.

"I'm newly attached to you and 'wither thou goest', and all that. Within reason." Seth gave a small smile. Sahara's eyes were shadowed, and he recognized the shock of losing his home, worry for his beloved friend.

"Hmmm." Sahara folded his arms, as if to say *bring it.* Seth couldn't wait to do just that. "What now?"

"Now we hang the white fairy lights—no cracks, please, way too obvious."

Sahara's lips quirked.

"Take the stepladder and kind of… weave them in amongst the displays. We'll save one set for the driftwood bed." Seth gave the fanciful bed a wistful look. It was the one he'd planned to give Sahara. But then he had an idea. "Never mind the fairy lights, I can do them.

Do you think you can take the bed upstairs and set it up in my—*our* room?"

"Oh, it's our room now, is it?" Sahara's voice was rough.

"Yes. Do you like it?"

Sahara ran a hand over the silvered, curling wood. "Yeah. Reminds me of the ocean."

SAHARA wasn't blind to Seth's workings; he knew the new bed was because he'd just lost his own—shit, everything. Just as he knew that Seth was building the holiday look like constructing a bright beacon. He was determined that this holiday would be special, determined to have faith that Toby would be a part of it.

If he hadn't already loved the man, loved him deeply and silently so that it felt as if he'd rip out part of his ribs if Seth needed one, this would have sealed the deal.

When he finished removing Seth's old bed and constructing the new one, he came downstairs to find Karen, Gecko, Karen's husband Fred, and Jared all helping with the holiday work. Seth was putting a necklace around Jared's neck. "Rose beads, made from summer rose petals. I cooked them up last fall."

"They smell…." Jared's dull eyes had a faint spark.

Seth smiled and squeezed Jared's hand. "Yes. Roses lift the spirits. I have another for you to take to Toby."

Jared's head fell. "Thanks."

Sahara and Gecko put out some special handmade menorahs that came from Quebec, Canada, nestling them amid more of Seth's gathered driftwood and the beach rocks he'd collected.

Despite everything, listening to Charlie Brown's Christmas music, Sahara found himself feeling a little lighter. It was being with friends, it was remembering what really mattered. He patted Jared's shoulder as he passed him sitting in front of a small altar with Kwan Yin.

When they were finished and the shop positively dripped like a wild fairy world of branches, flowers, candles, wool, silk, carvings, extracts and spices and dyes, Seth gave each helper a gift, insisting Jared take the best of his incense to burn in Toby's room if the hospital gave permission.

Then they walked back in a procession for the night watch, finding Toby's parents had disappeared from the waiting area. Heart pounding at this new development, Sahara accompanied Jared as they searched for them, finally finding them in the intensive care ward.

Toby's stepfather got up from a chair in the hallway and went to Jared with only a tiny hesitation. "They put him in a room. His mother's with him now. He asked for you, Jared. He opened his eyes and he asked, 'Where's my Jared?'"

Tears spilled from Jared's eyes. "I'll go see him."

MUCH later, in Seth's bedroom, Sahara closed the curtains before turning to watch Seth playing around with their Balinese lady. He wasn't sure why it had to be moved around on the table next to the bed. He'd just go *plunk* and that's all she wrote, but Seth....

"You're sure Gecko will be comfortable in a sleeping bag downstairs?" Seth asked.

Sahara nodded. "Don't worry. I'll spell him tonight on watch."

"I wish you didn't have to do that," Seth said.

Sahara shrugged. "It's okay."

"I'm so sorry about your home, all your things," Seth said, sitting down on the side of the bed he'd covered with some kind of gray linen. It was crisp and cool against the skin; Sahara decided he liked it.

"Just stuff. You're all right, Toby's going to pull through fine. What else matters? That shit you did tonight, getting everyone decorating, giving out those things. I feel like we had the real holiday."

Sahara undid his sarong and it fell, and his unsubtle erection was revealed fully, not that he hadn't been tenting the cloth ever since they'd climbed the stairs and entered the bedroom.

Seth gave him a shy, admiring glance, and his temperature shot up into the *hot* range. "Take that thing off," he ordered hoarsely.

Seth's eyes widened innocently. "What for?"

"So I can nail you into the mattress," Sahara replied. Then he blinked. Was that a romantic thing to say their first night together, new bed, new sheets?

But Seth didn't look displeased. He stood, and the cloth fell, revealing smooth, slim curves.

"You're mine," Sahara said, lifting Seth off his feet.

"Oh, yes," Seth agreed.

Chapter Twenty-Three

"I'M FEELING fine, really!" Toby protested when his mother wanted him to eat more of the waffles she'd smuggled in for him. "I'm totally full, so that's enough, Mom. And I'm getting out today. Hopefully soon!"

Seth shared an understanding look with his friend as his mother went in search of the nurse to see if he could leave as he hoped. Toby had been in the hospital a little over a week, mostly for observation, but they'd managed to repair the damage done and no infection had cropped up.

Now Toby was impatient to get back to his pool-cleaning job; Seth had learned that he was seriously considering buying out the elderly man who ran the service because he enjoyed it far more than he did starring on a gay soap. But Seth could see it. Toby was very down to earth. Or as Toby put it, "Now I *have* Jared. When I first started, it was the only way I could be close to him, though I couldn't admit that to myself for a very long time."

"I doubt you're going to be allowed to lift a finger at home," Seth said, smiling when Jared suddenly showed up with an orderly and a wheelchair. Toby let out a whoop.

"I think your rose beads helped," Jared said as an orderly assisted Toby into the chair. He was fully dressed, wearing a tie-dye blue T-shirt that Seth had made in one of his classes. "And also your daily visits. My guy is a little on the impatient side." There was an indulgent as well as sensual look in Jared's eyes.

"I want to go home and fu—" Toby closed his mouth, coloring.

Seth grinned. "Yeah, there is that."

Toby cocked his head at him as they headed down the elevator to where Sahara would be waiting. He and Seth had wanted to be there for their friends on this special day. "You sound pretty… relaxed."

"Nice euphemism."

"Uh-huh." Toby studied him. "I recognize *that* blush. Sahara is a fantastic lover!" Then Toby flushed again. "I mean, I guess he is."

"I know what you meant." Seth couldn't help grinning, remembering the last few nights—and some mornings and afternoons.

Sahara had insisted on filling in as his retail assistant in order to stay close by. Something about the way Seth and his friends had decorated the store the night Toby was out of the woods, some… atmosphere they'd all created together had resulted in the most successful season Seth had ever enjoyed in his fabric and dye shop, so he was frantically busy. He'd actually wound up selling even the waxed flowers and cream ware displays to a holiday bride. He'd be delivering them out to her home in the desert on Christmas Eve, after they closed for the day.

He hadn't mentioned this to Sahara, but it might mean that not only could he help out some of the artisans he worked with, he could also take some time off during the slower season in January or February, go sailing somewhere with his new lover.

So far Sahara hadn't talked about whether he was going to create another floating home. The remains of his last one were a write-off that had finally been cleared away. Sometimes he and Seth went down to the wharf in search of breakfast, and Seth saw the wistful glint in his blue eyes as he looked at the empty place on the pier.

But Seth didn't push. This was a wound, and Sahara needed time to heal before he could think what direction he wanted to take next.

In the meantime, they'd had a wild, happy afternoon of shopping for clothing for Sahara. Sahara looked hot in just about everything he tried on, and Seth loved him in his signature blue, so they'd picked up lots of T-shirts and light cotton sweaters in that color. His workplace had generously supplied him with more of the killer dark suits which set off his dazzling looks. When he strapped on his gun and put on a sports coat and a charcoal turtleneck, Seth wanted to drop to his knees and suck him off.

Mmmmm. He had done just that the other day, nearly making Sahara late for work. But it had been worth it, Sahara's hands tangled in his hair, Seth gripping his hips, his pants and silk boxers down just enough so Sahara could fuck his mouth.

And it had been both sexy and funny when Sahara rasped, "You really are turning into a good little cocksucker."

THE only thing that continued to cast a deep shadow was Rudy. Seth and Sahara had tried to lure him out with the ruse of Seth going somewhere "alone and helpless," but that hadn't worked. It didn't work if Seth pretended to be on his own in the shop after hours. Or walking down to the wharf at night, something he hadn't made a habit of before Rudy had crashed into his life.

Sahara was puzzled, but Seth felt that Rudy just *knew*. And so Sahara and Seth could never truly relax, because they knew he was out there. They knew he was patient and smart.

"YOU should go inside and rest," Jared scolded Toby later when all four friends sat out on the deck of their floating home.

"Jared, I just got here," Toby said, but he smiled, very gently, as if he could see the fear that still lived in his protective lover. "I'd really like some more chamomile tea; it might help me to nap later," he compromised.

Jared looked relieved, and Sahara felt for him. He couldn't imagine how he'd feel if Seth had been hurt as well. It had been hell enough when he'd gone missing. He knew Seth wouldn't like it, he'd get huffy or some shit, but Sahara saw himself as Seth's protector as much as Jared played the role for Toby.

"So have you decided if you're going to rebuild, Sahara?" Toby asked while Jared put the kettle on in the kitchen.

"I…." Now he hesitated, looking over at Seth. "I want to buy a sailboat, since I already, ah… well, I have somewhere to live at the moment." Sahara had insisted on picking up his living expenses, and Seth had been serene about it, just as if they'd decided from the beginning on the arrangement and not had it forced on them. It had made living with him so easy. And he liked the driftwood bed, and the strange containers that would arrive full of exotic treasures. He liked best of all being Seth's.

"Not just for the moment," Seth said. "I think a sailboat is a good idea, only… I get seasick."

"Not with me, you won't," Sahara said.

"Uh-huh." Seth didn't look convinced. "I'll go out with you anyway. I can take the same stuff I do when I go flying. Which I'll have to do right after the holidays are over anyway."

This was news to Sahara. "What?" He tensed.

"I, uh, have a special project I've been working on with some volunteer engineers," Seth said. "In one of the countries where I get my wood carvings, there is a lot of bleaching going on near a river." He looked at Toby and Jared, who had rejoined them, handing out tea to everyone. Even Sahara took it, though he grimaced a little at the chamomile. "Old clothing is being recycled, which is good, but the bleach is causing some real health problems. We may have found an alternative to implement."

"Just where is this?"

When Seth told him, Sahara swore.

"I've always been perfectly safe."

"Guess we'll both be going somewhere after the holidays," Sahara said darkly.

Damn him, Seth just smiled.

SAHARA knew he was no retail genius. He arrived home—ah, Seth's place—after a long stretch of protection duty. He hated to be away too long and always made sure either Gecko or someone else could be around to look after Seth.

So there he was, wearing his dark clothing, sunglasses, and gun, and he was wrapping pillows in holiday paper.

What he knew about folding paper was more the paper airplane variety than origami. And this stuff was blue (at least he liked the color) and waxy, hard to get just right. He winged it, though his gifts didn't look polished like the ones Seth and Karen produced. But hey, homemade was good, right?

"Maybe that's not your brand of paper," Seth noted. He squeezed Sahara's shoulder so he wouldn't take it as a criticism, smiling so Sahara knew he appreciated the help. Oh, man. Sahara was just nuts about him. He wanted the day to be over so they could walk down to the wharf and the sea breeze would stir those brown curls... or maybe they'd wind up in the special bed Seth had bought just for them, their bodies cooling and damp from the sex Seth's fantasy scenarios always inspired, with the window open to dry them off....

"I'll head to the shop across the street and get another kind," Seth offered. "Karen can man the till."

Sahara stiffened, not liking Seth out of his sight. He nodded to Gecko, and the man gracefully extricated himself from helping a customer and joined them.

"Seth duty."

Seth looked sheepish at the idea of his escort, but that was just tough shit.

Sahara would, by God, keep him safe.

"SO DO you ever hook up with someone when you're… you know, in town?" Seth asked Gecko as they crossed the street to the stationary shop. It was just getting ready to close, though it was bulging with customers in search of wrap and holiday cards.

"No, I'm celibate," Gecko said, looking unruffled by the crowd.

"Really?"

Gecko raised a reddish brow. "Weren't you? I thought you'd never… until Sahara."

Seth blushed. "Did he tell you that?"

"No, your scent changed."

Seth stared. "Excuse me?"

"I said, your scent changed."

Seth stopped searching through the remaining picked-over papers and folded his arms. "What, are you some kind of werewolf or something?"

Gecko gave a tiny grin. "Not hardly. I've just spent a lot of time hunting men. You smelled like linen sheets, like innocence, and then you smelled like Sahara."

"That's…." Seth didn't have the words. "I guess you're a hard guy to keep secrets from."

"Don't even try."

SETH didn't find enough of what he wanted, so when they returned, he gestured to the stairs. "I'm going to get some of last year's. I think it's in the linen cupboard."

Gecko hesitated, but Seth was already running up the flight. The store was packed. He had to get back and help out Karen and—

The knife pricked him under his chin. He caught his breath, staring into Rudy's eyes.

"Into your bedroom or I'll give you a second smile," Rudy ordered him in a colorless voice.

Heart pounding, Seth did as Rudy ordered, remembering Sahara had drilled him like one of his clients. *If the impossible happens, and he has you, do what he says until you think you have a chance. Just like you did with the truck, Seth. You hear me?*

In his bedroom, Seth swallowed thickly. Rudy kept crowding him, knife pricking into his skin so that warm blood ran down his neck. "You can't get away. The store is packed—"

"Yeah, useful." Rudy hefted a blond wig and hat in one hand so Seth could see them. "I made use of the holidays. Ho. Ho. Ho." He cocked his head. "What, Seth, you don't look like you have the spirit of the season?" Rudy jabbed him with the knife, and Seth stifled a cry, holding on, just like Sahara had told him. "You knew I'd come for you."

"I knew it," Seth agreed. He glared into Rudy's eyes. "And I hoped I'd get a chance to shove you into traffic or something."

"Not nice." Rudy played the tip of his blade against the oozing blood. "You're not a nice man, are you, whore?"

"I'm not a whore."

"Grow a pair, Seth? All these nights I thought Sahara had the only set in the family. You do let him tie you up." Rudy smirked. "That's right, I listened to you. The way you cry out. You like it when he puts it to you, don't you?"

Seth took a deep breath. "Just leave. He will kill you."

"I'm not afraid of him. I've been hunted before." Rudy's gaze became reflective. "I don't get you, why I was even interested in you. I never wanted a man before. I think it's something you did to me, all that stuff you write about."

"It was for *him*. I've been writing for Sahara almost from the first," Seth said. He was going to die, but he was going to die Sahara's man.

"After I'm done with you, I've been thinking how I'll dispose of the body," Rudy went on in a conversational tone. "You know, usually it's smart to cover your tracks, but I like the idea of Sahara finding you. Maybe I'll just leave what's left outside your shop."

Tears pricked Seth's eyes. *"No!"*

"Aw, you have a kind heart. I saw that when I put your friend in the hospital. Do you know I went in his room one night? He was sleeping, looked almost like an angel. I was all set to finish the job when his boyfriend showed up. They actually let them sleep together now in the same room. Lucky for your friend Toby, I guess."

Seth shivered. Rudy used the knife to make obscene little caresses against the side of his neck.

"Your heart is pounding so fast. So fast. Should I gag you and fuck you in the bed where he climbs on top of you? I saved myself for you."

"I won't let you."

"You think I don't have a backup plan?" Rudy put his mouth against Seth's ear. "Maybe I'll have to come back to this place when I'm done with you and... *boom*."

"Don't hurt anyone else," Seth growled. "It's me you want."

"It's you I want to hurt," Rudy said. "I'm going to cut you and put bruises on you, and by the time I'm done shoving shit up you, he won't want you."

An arm circled Rudy's neck. Rudy struggled, gurgling, the knife high, tip glinting in the light from the street.

There was a final-sounding *crack*, and Rudy fell like loose change into the hallway.

Panting, Seth stared at Sahara, taking in his hard face, his balled fists. He looked.... Seth threw himself into his arms.

Sahara lifted him, and Seth wrapped his legs around his hips. "Is he…?"

"He's not going to hurt anyone again," Sahara said.

Gecko appeared and took in the scene at a glance. "I'll call Martinez."

"Guess you'll have to close early," Sahara commented, taking Seth down the stairs. "I better take a look at those cuts on your neck."

Seth couldn't let go of his death grip. He was shaking, and Sahara was rubbing his back, slow, soothing circles. "You'd do anything to get out of wrapping any more gifts," he choked.

"You got that right," Sahara agreed.

Chapter Twenty-Four

GECKO couldn't hold his beer.

This was a revelation on a massive scale to Seth. He'd thought Gecko an impassive, on-the-small-scale Superman. With red hair.

But one beer and he gave Seth a sentimental smile from where he sat in the cockpit of Sahara's new sailboat. They'd left the pier around eleven, and now as the moon rose, Sahara anchored off a small cove. There was no sound but the wind and the tiny slap of moving water against the hull.

Seth breathed out a deep sigh of relief, basking in the peacefulness. It had been a very intense few months.

First, Martinez and Sahara had been able to trace Rudy back to a shack in the desert where he'd planned to take Seth. Sahara still wouldn't talk about what they'd found there, but he'd told Seth again that he was "fucking glad" he'd taken a nose dive out of that truck. They had also discovered a journal that might shed light on the disappearances of the two engineers in South America, and Seth was relieved for their families.

Then, early in the New Year, Seth left for his trip, but as Sahara had vowed, he did not go alone. Sahara had turned out to be a wonderful companion. He never lost patience or his sense of humor. He was as curious as Seth was about the various dyes made from local materials that had been in use for thousands of years. And he did not care about the primitive living conditions. He had a soft spot for village children. Because of his medic training, he was just as welcome a guest as Seth.

They relocated the workshop for the wood carvers, which took about a month, and Seth even encouraged some of the local women to consider forming a guild for their beautiful embroidery work. He bought as much of it as he could, turquoise silk with copper threads twisted into exotic designs, shipping it back to his store, where it was sure to be popular.

Seth had made a decision then, and when they'd returned, he'd given Karen the job of full-time manager of his shop. They hired someone part time to work with her, and Seth continued to manage the online business, but this freed him to enjoy more time with Sahara.

And Sahara needed him, because the nightmares were back.

He was not the cool, focused warrior who had killed to protect Seth. He was… lost. At first, Seth had almost missed it, but one day he noticed how often Sahara took solitary walks—usually in the middle of the night.

"I just go down to the wharf. It was my home for…." Sahara shrugged. "I like it down there."

Seth was rubbing his shoulders as the other man stripped off his jeans before getting into bed with Seth. Sometimes he made love to Seth almost furiously, as if he needed to forget himself.

"You had another nightmare," Seth said. "You don't deserve—"

"That's just bullshit and you know it." Sahara looked at him, reaching out to finger the blue beads Seth never removed. "It doesn't work that way."

"But you were better, weren't you?" Seth swallowed. "I mean, they weren't coming as often when we first got together."

Sahara shrugged.

Seth worried his bottom lip. It wasn't easy living with Sahara sometimes. The other man could bleed, but he wouldn't share it, silent. Seth looked up at the dreamcatcher hanging in the window that they'd made together after Rudy had kidnapped him, feeling a little guilty that for him, once Rudy was dead, the dreams had stopped coming. Of course, that could have just as much to do with having a big, protective, sandy-haired, macho ex-SEAL in his bed.

"Don't know," Sahara had muttered.

But Seth wouldn't leave it alone, and it wasn't long before he put two and two together. Sahara had said that living on the water helped with the nightmares, but he insisted he didn't want another floating home. However, he had talked about a sailboat.

They'd found a half-finished Sceptre 43 through the grapevine. It was a beautiful sailboat, built for cruising, and originally the owner had meant to finish all the teak inside it, but he'd passed away, leaving it on his widow's front lawn. She was more than happy to sell it to Sahara.

Gecko, Karen, Jared, and Toby, along with Seth, were there the day the mast was put on her and she was carefully lowered into the water. Sahara still had his old spot leased where his house had once been, so they moored her there.

He set up a small shack on the wharf with a saw and woodworking equipment and began to work on fitting her out, piece by piece, almost like a jigsaw puzzle.

Seth moved their Balinese lady aboard, saying one day they'd sail out there and see more of her kind.

And the first night that he slept with Sahara in their bunk in the bow, curled together, rocking gently, Sahara didn't have a single nightmare.

NOW Gecko rested his head back against the white fiberglass hull, where a compass and other equipment bulged next to a small window. Inside, they could hear Sahara rattling around with the dishes, washing up after a dinner of fresh seafood.

"This is nice, Seth. It was good of you to encourage Sahara to get this boat." Gecko smiled into his eyes, and for some reason, Seth felt his temperature shoot up a bit. Sheesh. Gecko was hot. Good thing Seth had Sahara, the man he loved, or he'd be crushing on the SEAL something fierce. "Hope you haven't turned into a sailing widow."

"Nah," Seth said. "I just take my laptop and go with him, whenever he wants to head out somewhere. Now that the weather is nicer, we may sail over to the Hawaiian Islands." Seth looked forward to that, as it was one place he'd never been. "Catch the Pineapple Express."

"Man, this is the life!"

"You need to sleep off that beer," Seth said, getting on his feet and going over to take Gecko's arm, trying to hoist him to his feet. "Come on, I'll get the extra berth ready for you to crawl in."

Gecko's eyes were heavy-lidded as he stared into Seth's. "Maybe I don't want to sleep," he muttered. "You smell…. Sahara's a lucky man, having you under him night after night."

Startled, Seth almost dropped his friend's arm. "You're wasted!"

"Nope."

"Sahara!" Sahara was there, of course he was there, but what Seth expected to happen, that he'd heft their friend downstairs, that they'd all wake up the next morning and nothing would be said… that's *not* what happened.

"It's your choice," Sahara said very softly, holding Seth's eyes. "You wrote about it so often, being with more than one man."

Seth stared at his lover in astonishment, heart pounding. "You wouldn't mind?"

"I had an arrangement once upon a time with Jared and Toby, remember? We'd do something, once in a while. Doesn't seem to have hurt any."

Seth swallowed, staring down at Gecko, who reached up and cupped Seth's face. "It's up to you, Seth. If it's no, we won't talk about it again."

Seth felt Sahara against his back. His bare chest, his hard arms around Seth protectively, the bulge of his erection, pressing against Seth's ass....

Gecko seemed to read him easily, just like always. He pulled Seth down into a kiss. He tasted of beer, and his tongue slipped inside Seth's mouth.

Seth shuddered, pulling away, looking at his two men for the night. He felt the way he had at the pavilion, wild, free, *hot*.

SETH moaned when Sahara's hands worked under his T-shirt, teasing his nipples. Gecko was kissing his neck, his hand running down to cup Seth appreciatively through his shorts, stroking his erection. "We're going to use you so good," he whispered. "Just like that stuff you write about."

Seth's joy in his writing had been a little subdued since Rudy, even with Sahara's enjoyment of his fantasies. His eyes popped open. "You read my blog?"

"Are you kidding? I told you I'm celibate, not dead. You are smoking, Seth."

Sahara slid his shorts and boxers off, and Gecko removed his T-shirt. Both his men seemed to want him naked, right now, sandwiched between them.

For a second under the moonlight, he was aware of his slight body, of his pale skin that wouldn't tan no matter how often he went out on the boat with Sahara, but then Gecko's hands tangled in his curls, bringing him close for another scorching kiss, and he whimpered as his needy erection rubbed against the other man.

Sahara was kneading his bottom the way he liked, pinching the skin and then ghosting a finger down his crevice, exciting him.

"I really think you need to suck our guest off, Seth," Sahara suggested mildly. "It's only hospitable."

"Fuck!" Seth fell to his knees, running his hands over Gecko's muscular, freckled legs. Sahara knelt behind him, and he felt the press of lubed fingers in his opening. Oh, he was going to get it, all right.

He and Gecko rushed to get his belt open, and then they both laughed when their heads collided. "Ouch," Gecko complained.

"Sit back," Seth commanded, that heady *I'm flying* feeling moving through him. It helped that his man was behind him, Sahara Blue, the most beautiful man he'd ever seen, the man he'd wanted so long. Now his lover was giving him a fantasy, just for Seth, probably to put to rest any fears that Seth might still hold that he wasn't attractive.

Seth could have told him that after months in his bed, he didn't need that anymore. Anyone who lay under Sahara, sometimes more than once a night, body worn out and achy from being pounded, damn well knew he was wanted.

Sahara could barely keep his hands off him.

Seth tugged down Gecko's shorts, and his eyes widened at what he revealed. Gecko was not a big guy. He was much shorter than Sahara but… wow.

"I think it might be as thick as my wrist. And is that a…?"

Gecko blushed, the color almost as fiery as his dark red hair. "A tattoo, yeah. Don't ask. It was stupid shit, a dare."

"I can't wait to taste you," Seth said honestly, and Gecko cried out "Holy *fuck!*" when Seth swallowed him, humming his approval.

Seth felt a familiar thick pressure against his opening. Sahara hadn't fingered him. He wanted to give him just that edge of pain that Seth liked sometimes. He pushed in, steady, and Seth released Gecko's cock, gasping.

"Oh, fuck, you are so hot. Look at you take it!" Gecko whispered, his hand, Sahara's hand, tangled in Seth's hair.

As Sahara began to ride him, Seth spread himself wider, allowing his lover access to go as deep as he wanted.

"I think you need to get back to work." Gecko brushed his lips with his erection, and Seth felt his balls tighten. He was going to come soon. Come without any touch to his neglected penis, just the way he liked it sometimes.

Seth obediently dipped over Gecko's cock, sucking hard on his shaft. He pulled away and decided to share his fantasy with his two men. "Maybe this is my first night in some kind of futuristic prison. And Sahara is the dark, dangerous prisoner everyone is afraid of. He usually watches guys he likes with other men, but tonight when I went down on you in our cell, he couldn't keep from—Ah!"

Gecko's eyes widened, and he panted, "Oh, shit, I'm going to.... It's been too long!"

"Do it on his face," Sahara growled, very much the dark, dangerous figure of Seth's fantasy. "I want to see it."

Seth gave Gecko a teasing lick, and the other man groaned, muscles tightening, head thrown back as his semen hit Seth's chin, his lips. Seth gripped Gecko's thick thighs as Sahara pounded into his prostate, indirectly giving him all he needed to—

When he clenched around Sahara, groaning out the long contractions of his pleasure, Sahara snarled a hand possessively in his hair and pulled his head back. He bit the side of his neck, leaving a mark, while his other hand went to the dangling pendant. He crushed it in his hand, possessive.

THE next morning when Seth woke up, he was tangled with Sahara out on the deck of their boat. He rubbed his morning beard, yearning for coffee. Although he hadn't had more than a beer to drink, he felt slightly hung-over… and well-used.

Sahara's lips closed over his erection, and Seth hummed his approval as his lover sucked him. Okay, the coffee could wait.

"I'd fucking give you one of my ribs," Sahara said as he lifted Seth up so he could take more of him.

Sahara translation: *I love you, Seth.* Smiling, Seth gave himself completely to his lover.

"NO SIGN of Gecko," Seth said later, after a dip in the ocean with Sahara. Sahara had coffee and eggs waiting for him in the cockpit, which he dug into, ravenous. *Nothing like a threesome to stir a man's appetite*, he thought. And then, *Wow! Plain, boring, mousy Seth Hollis had a threesome.*

"He wouldn't have wanted to impose," Sahara said with a shrug. "Probably dived over and swam to the beach, hitched a ride home."

Sahara settled down behind Seth and held him while he finished his breakfast. Although Sahara had had him just an hour before, Seth felt familiar hardness nudging his backside. They were insatiable for each other, white hot.

"I saw you brought your laptop," Sahara murmured, his sandy eyelashes shielding his gaze from Seth.

Seth made a quizzical sound, looking up at his lover. Sahara didn't make idle conversation. In fact, some days, Seth had to thump him to get him to open up and talk at all.

"Yeah, I always do," Seth said, loving Sahara's arms around him, the way he rubbed Seth's thigh below his shorts, the rasp of his morning beard against Seth's cheek when he nuzzled him.

"This will probably sound crazy…."

"Hmm?"

"I just want to pull up anchor and head out somewhere. She's fully stocked," Sahara said. "Has been for weeks. Water, food… and we can pick our kitten up from the shop."

Seth turned around to face Sahara. "Where would we go?"

Sahara shrugged. "No idea. Does it matter?"

And Seth fingered the pendant he wore, the blue beads the same color of his lover's eyes. "No," he said. "It doesn't matter."

Epilogue

SETH had turned out to be a fair sailor, once he'd gotten over his habitual seasickness. Musing over that, Sahara stepped up from the galley to the deck of their sloop, finding his lover curled into a little ball on the fiberglass bench, sleeping, only his brown curls moving in the wind. Their cat, who had turned into a watch cat and didn't let any other felines near their boat when they were moored somewhere, was licking his paws serenely in the shade from the awning Sahara had strung up as protection for Seth's delicate skin; even after weeks at sea, the man continued to burn, not tan.

"I'm not asleep," Seth said in a sleepy voice. "I'm on watch with Lotus. I'm actually just resting my eyes."

"Uh-huh," Sahara said, feeling like smiling. Seth always made him feel this way. They had experienced some rough weather on their voyage to the Hawaiian islands, a real shakeout cruise, but one night when the waves were crashing over their bow and Sahara was working to bring in the torn canvas of their main sail, he'd suddenly realized he hadn't had a nightmare in a few nights. He was exhausted, browned, exhilarated.

He was in love.

Seth had spent a lot of that period sick as the proverbial dog until he'd finally, *finally* gotten his sea legs and the illness had let up. Good thing, too, since Sahara had been worried about him and seriously considered having him picked up by the Coast Guard when he'd lost so much weight.

"So where to this morning, Captain?" Seth asked, sitting up and rubbing his bed hair. He looked adorable… and sexy. He was wearing a sarong, this one patterned with island orchids.

"I was thinking the Valley of the Temples. The Byodo-In Temple."

Seth's eyes widened with enthusiasm. Sahara knew he'd been wanting to go there, the beautiful Japanese Buddhist complex built in honor of the first Japanese emigrants to the islands.

The day before, they'd traveled high up into the mountains on the island of Oahu, seeing cactus growing on ground that looked blasted. Sahara had seen it before when he'd been stationed briefly on the island, but it was all new to Seth. They'd even gathered bits of loose lava rock and purchased a small mask of the sea god Kanaloa to incorporate into a new dreamcatcher for their sailboat. Seth said he was taking no chances with Sahara having bad dreams again.

"How's the shop doing?" Sahara asked, as he did every day. He knew Seth appreciated it.

"Karen recruited Jared and Toby to help with the look. They've got a great design sense, so I think it'll be helpful for the upcoming sale. Plus, Toby finally convinced Jared he was all clear to work full time again."

"He likes to keep him safe."

"Toby would say he's a tad too overprotective."

"Mmm." But Sahara could relate to feeling that way. And recently he'd been in touch with Jared himself—specifically looking for recommendations on the islands for a goldsmith who made Polynesian-inspired jewelry. He brushed his hand against the little box in his shorts pocket which carried two titanium and Koa wood rings. When he and Seth got to the temple later, he had something he wanted to ask him.

JAN IRVING has worked in all kinds of creative fields, from painting silk to making porcelain ceramics, to interior design, but writing was always her passion.

She feels you can't fully understand characters until you follow their journey through a story world. Many kinds of worlds interest her, fantasy, historical, science fiction and suspense—but all have one thing in common, people finding a way to live together—in the most emotional and erotic fashion possible, of course!

Visit Jan's blog at http://jan-revealed.livejournal.com and her web site at http://janirvingwrites.com/.

Also by JAN IRVING

http://www.dreamspinnerpress.com